When Irish Eyes Are Crying

by

Stephen D. Manning

This is a work of fiction. Any resemblance of any of the characters to persons living or dead is strictly coincidental.

FIRST EDITION

Copyright 1997, by Stephen D. Manning
Library of Congress Catalog Card No: 96-90583
ISBN: 1-56002-693-6

UNIVERSITY EDITIONS, Inc.
59 Oak Lane, Spring Valley
Huntington, West Virginia 25704

Cover art by Jennifer Wentworth
Cover design by Julia Lucas

Dedication

To my family and friends,
anyone who has suffered from mental illness and its stigma
and to the kind professionals who feel compelled to help.

Chapter One

In essence it would be nearly impossible for me to relay every detail of my story. Indeed, father time has blotted out many details that may turn out to be pertinent to this text. It is time, and time alone, that has blurred some of my vision. Let it suffice to say, what you are about to read is a true, factual account. I am writing for two reasons. One, it is extremely therapeutic for myself. Two, I'm hoping the reader will be enlightened on the subject of manic-depression and all it entails. I fervently hope it will be as enlightening to you as it is therapeutic for me.

First and foremost, allow me to introduce myself. My name is Archie McRae and I am a twenty-seven year old caucasian male of Irish descent. I have similar background and interests of a typical American male. I am single, between jobs (like about 800 million other American males in this time of repression), have no girlfriend and no money. I tell you this so that you know that I have time on my hands enough to write, at length, my story.

I was born in Chester, Pennsylvania to a man and woman who were to be divorced shortly after my birth. I have two older sisters, Marty (Martha) and Kim. Marty is four years older than me and Kim is three and a half years older than me. We were raised, solely, by my mother from the time I was an infant to the time I was ten years of age when she married Ken, her boyfriend of long standing. Ken, a strong influence in my life, was a radio officer for an oil company and spent half of his time at sea. Needless to say, most of my early influence was that of female persuasion. I have friends who say that this is the root of all of my problems. Of course, this is the male sexist view, but I rule out nothing in way of explanation.

I'm not saying there were no male role models or males who played major roles in my life. In fact, I had as many friends to play ball with as the next guy and I had an older cousin, Mark, who served not only as friend but also as a brother type figure. Also, my father always lived nearby and would take me to sporting events almost every weekend. By about the time I could walk, I was a sports addict. This is the reason why I had so many delusions about sports figures, which you will read about shortly.

That is if you don't get bored or throw up all over this text. So, I grew up a natural and healthy specimen. Well, almost healthy. Okay, I had a few problems.

Let's just say my medical portfolio was spotty at best. I was a severe anemic, I had a heart murmur, a slight hole in my heart, was easily susceptible to colds and flue, had my spleen removed following a near fatal sledding accident, and most importantly to this text, although I was sickly, I was extremely hyperactive. This suggests to me that I suffered from childhood depression but was never diagnosed.

Before I divulge my story, it is important to note that I thought I had a normal childhood. Indeed, I was very normal, much like I am now, but things changed when I reached the age of fifteen. This is where my story begins.

The year previous to my fifteenth, my freshman year in high school, I was a "straight A" student at a highly respected Catholic high school in the suburbs of Philadelphia, Pennsylvania. I was living with my father and two sisters in a little, old duplex in Darby, Pennsylvania. My mother and stepfather had moved to Huntington Beach, California the year previous and I spent a lonely year there with very few friends. I had decided that I wanted to return to the Philadelphia area and receive the best education possible. Indeed, this was a very good decision, as I excelled in school and out. I was very active with friends, I played about four hours of basketball a day, and I studied very hard at night. All my reports to California were that I was doing fantastic at everything. But along came my sophomore year, my fifteenth, a year that was going to change me forever.

From the opening day of school in September, to the mid of February I was visited by a hideous beast known as indogenous depression. This beast disrupted my life so much that you could say that it actually destroyed me.

For starters, the depression lets itself be known in the most basic aspects of human existence. For instance, everything we humans take for granted is disrupted. Eating becomes a painstaking chore, if indeed you chose to eat. Often times when you do eat, your nervous stomach churns and rejects the offering. Sleeping is even worse. Although you have an overwhelming desire to sleep, if you have agitated depression, which is what I had, sleeping is a virtual impossibility. Of course, you do pick up some sleep, but for the most part you lie in bed, panic stricken in pools of your own sweat, wishing you were dead. In my particular case, every moment I could spare was spent in bed trying to find solace from the hideous beast that coursed my veins. I was unsuccessful most of the time.

During the first month of the school year it was painfully obvious that I was well on my way of failing out of school. The prior year I had worked my way to the top echelon of the school and in one month all of my hard work had been destroyed. I could not study for I could not concentrate. The best grade I remember receiving in that first month was 40 out of 100. The prior year, my average was 95 out of a 100. Needless to say, my parents started to become very concerned. My poor father had no clue as to what to do with me. He was so frustrated that the only thing he could do was suggest that I be sent back to California. This was his only recourse, actually, for he thought what was missing in my life was my mother. So I went, not just to appease my father but to try to kill the beast that had its grips on me.

My depressive days in Pennsylvania were frightening to say the least. I walked through life panic stricken. I feared everything and lost interest in everything as well. I no longer had the desire to play ball or hang out with my friends. I had no confidence in myself or anything else. Uncertainty was my middle name. One time my Uncle Jay asked me, "How are you laddybuck?" My reply was, "I . . . I . . . I don't know." He looked at me dumbfounded. I wasn't certain how to answer that question just like I wasn't certain of anything else.

The best way I can describe the depression, assuming you have normal mental health, is to tell you to take your worst depression and multiply it by ten. Then, you have to live with that for weeks sometimes months on end. In my particular case, the depression, all tolled, lasted four solid months. Four solid months of an agitated depression in which there is a constant throbbing sensation as if I could feel the blood coursing my veins at all times. It was hideous. Why I continued to live I have no idea. Or yes I do, I could visualize my mother crying at my funeral. This visualization is the only thing that saved my life.

The day before I escaped to California, I sat sullen on the bus home from school. Next to me was my cousin Mark who attended the same school. He and I were very close and I was thinking about how much I was going to miss him. It began to pour down rain in droves and he tried to console me by saying, "at least you won't have to put up with this shit anymore." As I watched the downpour, I almost began to cry. I had been good at hiding my tears in public, but this time it was almost unbearable. The thought of missing my family and friends devastated me. My heart screamed not to go but I had no choice. It was as if I were a bullet locked in the chamber. The busride home was a sad farewell to my dear, vital companion Mark. I knew I would see him again at Christmas and summer but I also knew our lives would change and the bond we had would loosen.

The day I left, I went to school as usual. As usual I got nothing out of class, my mind focused on my pain. I missed the bus going home for some reason and I had to take the trolley to a neighboring town. It was October 10th and believe it or not, it began to snow. I walked a mile home in the snow. It was a walk that I'll never forget. I froze my hands off holding an umbrella and books and all the while I was panic stricken fearing I'd never get home alive. As I trudged, I thought the snow said something to me. It said, "it's time to leave boy." Yes, indeed it was time for me to leave. My only hope was that my new life in the sun would lift my depression.

    The sun did not lift my depression. All it did was make me hate the sun. But I had to make the best of my new life as much as possible. Of course I was enrolled in school but enrolling was an ordeal in itself. I had lived in California for a year in the eighth grade and I had acquired a few close friends. They were all going to a neighboring school which was farther from the school closest to my house. I had my choice between the schools and in true depressive form, I hemmed and hawed mercilessly until I finally decided to go to the school closest to my home. The school that none of my friends would be attending. This decision was made so that I didn't have to face any of my old friends in my condition. I was hiding, isolating myself. I gave the excuse that I wanted to start anew, but I was really quite ashamed of the way I was and didn't want anyone who knew me to see me.

    The first couple of months at the new school saw me struggling and I honestly thought it would take me eight years to graduate. The school had a system in which you worked at your own pace. They gave you packets of material, each of which had to be successfully completed before you move on to the next. I was in a panic at first, and the first couple of those packets took forever to complete. I thought I would never survive. Indeed, my depression was so bad at this point, the chances of suicide were increasing drastically. The very idea that you couldn't advance unless you passed a previous packet was enormous pressure for someone who had severe depression and anxiety attacks about what socks to wear to school. I muttled through, though, with luck and divine intervention. Believe me, divine intervention does exist, otherwise I would not be at this keyboard.

    Before my depression finally subsided, as I mentioned earlier, I had many thoughts of suicide. I was particularly obsessed with the butcher knives in the kitchen. Running yourself through seemed like such a natural thing. Why not? What else was there to live for but another day of the hideous beast? Yet every time I eyed those knives the vision of my mother crying at my funeral lept forward and clutched me from the jaws of death. I desperately wanted to leave my misery and rise to a higher ground, but that vision wouldn't let me.

    A point of note as to when and how the depression stopped. It stopped rather abruptly after a four month reign. How it stopped is interesting. One would think that because it was biologically based there would be no external stimulus that could trigger a cease fire in the depression. There was.

One night while studying at the dining room table, my stepfather, Ken, stood above me and gave me an inspirational talk. In a sincere, reverent tone he spoke, "Archie, I want to talk to you. I want you to know that your mother and I love you at all costs. You don't have to be a 'straight A' student for us to love you. You don't need to put so much pressure on yourself to succeed. If that takes any off the pressure off of you then it was well worth saying. We just want you to be happy and healthy again."

That speech took a lot of pressure off me and I moderately began my ascent to better health. It was the most pivotal statement in my recovery, quite possibly in my life.

Chapter Two

The next few months, from February to the end of the school year, I had returned to the Archie of old, a young man who collected a wholesome batch of friends and great grades. My obsession with sports and girls had returned in spades and it would be safe to say that I was as healthy as any other all American boy. At least it seemed as if I was healthy. Little did I know at this point that I was only experiencing the normal phase of the manic depressive cycle. This stage can be likened to that of the eye of a hurricane. The first stage of the storm was over but the second stage was to come with much more force and verve.

During this time I was very active. I was studying relatively hard, as hard as a bum like me can study, about four minutes a day or seven if I applied myself. I was also playing a lot of basketball. This I was very serious about, playing as much as four hours a day. I played spring league ball with the junior varsity team and I was doing very well except for the fact the coach didn't give me much playing time. It may have been due to my stature (5'4") or it may have been that I was the new kid on the block. Regardless, either explanation, I was getting pretty discouraged on the bench after doing well in practice against guys twice my size. I had worked as hard, if not harder than the others, and if I might say myself, I made some of the starters look pretty bad everyday in practice. I deserved to get some playing time and I sat on the bench. It was only spring league, we were the best team in the county, we were beating teams by thirty to forty points and there I was riding the pines, wondering if Maria, a cute little Mexican girl who spoke no English, would go bowling with me. Maybe Gatney (the coach) didn't like me. All I know is that I got one chance to strut my stuff. It was late in the last game and we were blowing out the opposing team by an enormous differential. There was about two and a half minutes left in the game and their starters were still aboard. I scored four points, dished two wonderfully aesthetic assists, ripped off their star twice for precious steals, and even blocked a shot of a guy who stood about six feet tall. I certainly caught the attention of everyone but it was to be the first and last game I played for the school. They wanted me to play summer league ball but I was headed back to Philadelphia to see my father and old chums. They said I would have a tough time making the team in the fall if I missed summer league. So be it, my loved ones are more important.

Around the time of the last game I obtained my California driver's license. Yes indeed, nothing like a hyperactive snot like myself with license to boom down California freeways. Just what the good citizens of the golden state needed—another punk on the road blasting Neil Young tunes, thinking he knows everything. Actually I was, and still am, a good safe driver. Interesting note however: a manic depressive sometimes drives according to his or her mood. If he or she is depressed he or she may tend to drive slow and over cautious, fearing a bug farting on the windshield. If he or she is in the normal range, he or she drives normally. If he or she is completely manic, he or she may get to meet Mr. Officer. Anyway, at this point in time, I was driving safely.

The summer was great. I hung out with a batch of friends that I'd known since the first grade. They are the same batch of friends I have to this day. That, of course, is testimony to them. We played basketball and went camping down at Avalon campgrounds in New Jersey. The most important note of the summer, however, was that I fell in love for the first time. I had been infatuated by many girls in school but nothing that compared to Maureen around the corner from my dad's house in Darby. She was beautiful, smart and fun to be around. One problem, she was a couple years younger than me and had never kissed a boy before. I took her bowling on her first date and we had a great time. Afterwards, we ate ice cream or something, she said yes. Whoooopie! I was her first kiss but she was not mine. Nonetheless, she was the first girl I ever really cared about and although we cooled the relationship down after only a few sweet kisses, we became close, lifelong friends. I'm happy to say she's still my friend after eleven years of separation. I'm awfully proud to be her friend.

During the course of the summer, I suppose my pace was that of a hypomanic which is the productive phase before full blown mania. I had a great deal of energy but not so much as to be considered abnormal by others. During this time I should have been more creative but was not. I did not partake in my favorite hobby of writing. I was just another kid out for fun. It's an interesting note that some manic depressives display hypergraphia when in the hypomanic state. We just love to write for no apparent reason other than the simple enjoyment of seeing what comes out of our heads. I write poetry, journals and even wrote half a screenplay when I was fourteen. I firmly believe that hypergraphia is a byproduct of the illness itself, but it is extremely difficult when mother depression rears her ugly head.

The summer of nineteen eighty came to an abrupt halt and with its end came the sad goodbyes that I had grown accustomed to but never enjoyed. I'm lucky in the sense that I had opportunity to see old friends but I'm unlucky in the sense that I always had to say goodbye to them. It's an ugly affair. At the ripe age of sixteen I led a dualistic life. I was essentially bi-coastal and had never made a dime in my life. I had two sets of friends and lived in two drastically different environments with different cultures and social mores. I suppose if I had to say so, I am a Pennsylvanian living in California. I don't like or dislike one more than the other but since most of my family is now in California, it is here that I stay. Just call me a Pennacalifavian.

I said my painful goodbyes and packed my bags—destination: the land of fruits and nuts. There were plenty of fruit trees but the only nut I saw was standing in the mirror. School was once again school. I had been a member of the model U.N. and in October (the eighth to be precise) we had our first conference at the University of California in San Diego. This marked the beginning of my first manic episode. It was to be the first of many, unfortunately, and it could quite possibly be considered the grand daddy of them all. It's duration was approximately a month and it was one twisted sister.

We arrived at the conference and we were supposed to meet with other delegates of our countries to discuss strategy. My country was Yemen, a third world country in Africa, and I figured it this way; nobody listens to third world countries anyway, so I might as well have fun. We had arrived at the conference an hour early, 8:00 A.M., and I decided to stray from the herd and check out the acoustics of the lecture hall where the main conference was to be held. I had brought with me a harmonica and Neil Young's "Decade" songbook. I snuck into the massive, empty lecture hall, went down to the front where the microphones were and began whaling away on my harmonica, singing Neil Young tunes at the top of my lungs. I thought I was doing a pretty decent job, but when you're completely manic, you think you can do things you really can't do. Our M.U.N. teacher, Mr. Bosley, who apparently had an all points bulletin posted for me, finally caught up with me and nailed me to the wall. He came in through the back of the lecture hall, eyes ablazing, "Archie!! what in God's name do you think you're doing!!?" I proudly retorted with a big, big smile, "I'm checking out the acoustics by singing a few choice tunes," I continued to smile. He snapped out, "I want you to get out there and meet with your country!!"

I sheepishly complied and met with my country. It took me nanoseconds before I mesmerized the other delegates, "Alright boys (some of them were girls) here it is. We're a third world country and we ain't gonna get shit out of no one, so what do you say we kick back and catch a few Z's!?" (A Knute Rockne speech if ever there was one.) The other delegates, mouths agape, didn't think My plan was a good one. However, since I knew everything, I followed my game plan pretty much to the T. I did no homework for this conference thinking M.U.N. was only a social club, and I had myself a fairly good time. However, the other kids from my country, from other schools, didn't heed my advice and tried to get every award the conference offered. I was proud of my teammates and their diligence, but being manic, I almost, single handedly, blew it for all of them. This is how it happened.

I was a delegate in the Economic and Social council. Most of the morning was spent flirting and clowning around with the cute blonde sitting in front of me. She was the delegate from Cameroon which was odd since I had never heard of a blonde beauty from Cameroon. We had ourselves a wonderful time laughing and joking. We had so much fun, in fact, that the chairman had to insist that she quiet her laughter. It was at this point that I decided that Yemen was to be heard from in a serious vein. It was time for me to Economize and Socialize with the Economic and Social council. I went to the front of the room to the microphone and delivered a speech that blew the stack off of Damion Cutler, one of my many very serious classmates. Instead of discussing the issue at hand, I said (I remember this verbatim) "it seems to me that everyone who's come up front here is really uptight. Just relax, take it easy." I blew the mind of everyone in the large room. The chairman of the committee looked at me stunned, bewildered, and not entirely amused, "Thank you Yemen." I cordially returned his thanks, "you're welcome sir."

When I returned to my seat, Damion Cutler was waiting for me with a full head of steam. He dragged me into the hallway and chewed me out as only blubber boy could. "Archie! I don't care if you want to blow this for yourself but for God's sake don't blow it for the rest of us who have worked so hard to win awards!" How could I take a guy like Damion Cutler seriously? He weighed four tons and drool was spilling from his big ass lower lip. I didn't say another word for the remainder of the conference. In fact, I left. I walked all over campus and then I walked off campus. I ran across a highway with cars whizzing past me and honking horns. I walked through a huge business complex looking for a bathroom but every office was closed on Saturday. So, I stood on top of a hill with a wonderful view of San Diego, put my hand in my shirt, imagined I was Napoleon, and urinated on the city of San Diego.

Of course, now, the city of San Diego was officially McRae land. X marks the spot babe. All kidding aside, I was in sort of gray area here. I was behaving very erratically on this day, doing things I could never imagine myself doing. I don't urinate in public in broad daylight. I don't think I'm Napoleon. I don't run across highways with cars whizzing by and honking. I don't let idiots like Damion Cutler bother me. I don't make half assed speeches in front of a room full of people. I don't even flirt with cute blondes—I'm too shy. The yellow flag was waving in the wind.

When I finally calmed down after the Cutler ordeal, I made my way back to the conference room only to discover that everyone had re-assembled in the main lecture hall. I had been gone for hours just walking around entertaining my wild imagination. I peeped in and decided I'd wait out the remainder of the conference on the bus. Indeed, I went and sat on the bus only to find some fun in the sun dude playing basketball on the courts next to the bus. Being that I was impulsive and all, I decided to take Mr. Surfer to the cleaners. I walked out on the court wearing suit and tie, and cowboy boots a size too small for me (I'm not fond of cowboy boots but they were the only shoes I had dressy enough for the conference).

"Do you mind if I shoot around with you?" I shouted from about half court.

"Yes I do mind," he shouted back. Mr. San Diego was a rude bastard.

"Do you want to play one on one?" I know I did.

Mr. San Diego snickered.

"I've got five bucks here that says I can beat you up to ten," I showed him the five bucks.

"Alright high school boy, let's party" Mr. San Diego was cocky.

I estimated Mr. San Diego to be a junior or senior in college which would make him about twenty-one or twenty-two years of age. He was about six feet one or two inches tall and wore no shirt revealing his tanned, well developed physique. If I weren't painfully heterosexual I would be making a pass at Mr. San Diego rather than playing ball against him.

He shot for outs from the top of the key and the ball was received by nothing but net. If I hadn't been a touch maniacal and delusional at the time, I would have been concerned about my five bucks. He started in by using the cheapest trick in the book—he'd back me up with his ass, get right under the hole and shoot over me for an easy bucket. We the little people of basketball hate this tactic. He did this six times in a row (we were playing winners outs) until finally he missed and I snagged the rebound. Then I went off like a lit candle. I hit the first one from the top of the key, drove the lane for the second and then bombarded him with long guided missiles that precisely hit the mark. The game was up to ten and I had nailed nine straight. Mr. San Diego was in big trouble. Little did I know at the time,

I was in trouble as well. While we had been playing, the other kids had been filing onto the bus. When the score had reached nine-six my favor, I heard my friend Randy scream out the window, "hurry up and make short of this bozo, Bosley's been searching for you all day!" Sure enough, I'm getting ready to shoot my last shot from the top of the key and the boss man is headed straight for me and he was bringing the mother load. I hit my victory shot, ran over to pick up my jacket off the grass and hustled my cute little behind onto the bus and parked in the only available seat on the bus next to sophomore, Bobby Raymond.

I was sweating like a pig and panting like a dog when Bosley ran onto the bus, ran down the aisle and started screaming in my face. A quick word on Mr. Bosley: he had been an acid dropping, dope smoking hippie boy in the sixties. He constantly yammered on about peace and free love and all that silliness. It got a tad old when you were an adolescent of Nineteen Eighty. But we had to listen to it because he was our teacher and an intellectual who thought he knew everything. There was one thing he did not know and that was where I had been for the last few hours. He tore into me good. "Archie you little son of a bitch! Where have you been?! I looked all over campus for you the past three hours!" I said nothing and sat staring at him almost in tears. "You are the biggest disappointment in this program! You have as much potential if not more than anyone on this bus! But all you choose is to fuck off!" With that he turned around and went to sit in his seat at the front of the bus. The bus was dead silent for ten minutes as we rolled and there were tears welling up in my eyes. He actually called my mother a bitch and used the "f" word. Have you ever heard a teacher say those words to a student? I hadn't. Particularly not to me. I assumed after that moment that Bosley and I weren't going to be putting on the beads together or smoking the peace joint. I certainly wasn't going to flash him the peace sign the next time I passed him in the hall. Maybe I could muster up the energy to give him half the peace sign but not the whole thing, man.

Eventually the other kids started talking and clowning around. We, as a school, did very well at the conference, snaking many accommodations and a few gavels which was the top award. Bobby Raymond had won one and he was only a sophomore. I complimented him on his feat and he replied in kind claiming he never knew I could play basketball as well as I could. Almost immediately I had forgotten about the Bosley ordeal and started joking around with my new buddy Bobby. On our two hour trip back to Huntington Beach, Bobby and I wrote a seven verse song called "Yoda Lives." It was a tribute to the George Lucas' Character Yoda who was a favorite in "The Empire Strikes Back." I'd write out the whole thing but I only remember the first verse after all these years:

> He's the oldest living master
> our savior from disaster
> he's Yoda,
> Yoda lives.

All the verses ended in he's Yoda, Yoda lives. Bobby and I had a whale of a good time on the way home. He had won a major award and I had urinated on the city of San Diego claiming it as my own. All in all not a bad day. Man 'o man o' man, I was as high as a kite due to my mental disorder and barbs with the likes of Cutler and Bosley pales to the memory of my mood on that particular day. I accomplished absolutely nothing productive on that day and I felt great! (By the way, Mr. San Diego, if you ever read this, you owe me five bucks plus 6% interest—that's compounded daily dear.)

The next three weeks, following the conference, found me creeping into an intense manic high. The yellow flag was no longer waving, it had been replaced by the red flag. I was rapidly entering the black zone—the point of no return. During those few weeks I was functional and wasn't thoroughly aware that my energy level was increasing. I was eating and sleeping regularly for the most part but I did notice, however, that I was staying up later listening to the same two albums. One was "Live Rust" by Neil Young and the other was "Late for the sky" by Jackson Browne. "Live Rust" was upbeat and was always played first and "Late for the sky" was very mellow and lyrically soothing and always served well as a nightcap. Staying up, listening to these albums, didn't seem to affect how I functioned during the day. So, the increase in emotional energy went unnoticed even by myself. It is possible, now that I'm a veteran of the disorder, to notice such changes in energy but even now, it is difficult to stop the deluge. At that particular point in time I was a rookie and was completely unaware of what was happening to me. A storm was coming and I was unprepared.

The storm came the first two weeks of November and lasted quite a while. Interestingly, the month of November causes me great heartache to this day. When the days get shorter I either find myself becoming manic or depressed. On this year, 1980, I was to become manic. The previous year found me severely depressed. There is no telling which way I'll go on any given year, but the month of November usually finds me crawling inside my skin trying to hide from the beast. I don't come out until I'm used to the changes nature has brought. I have experienced episodes of mania and bouts of depression at other times of the year, but I do most of my hiding the first week of November every year, due to bad old memories and an overwhelming feeling of impending doom.

Before I recount the events of this week, allow me to give you an overview on my state of being. First of all, my energy level had increased to the point where I was no longer able to sleep. My mind was racing increasingly into the night. The thoughts (or should I say delusions) were usually thoughts of superiority. I was the smartest kid in school and I could do anything. Blah, blah, blah. I could, and was, magically solving every earthly problem while lying in my bed wide awake. This was my divine purpose, God had sent me to solve every problem man encounters.

My diet consisted of saltine crackers and an enormous amount of iced tea. When I sat down to eat a meal, my stomach became magically queasy and I would wind up eating practically nothing. I had always had a nervous stomach, had frequently vomited meals as a youngster and me not eating during this week or two, simply went unnoticed by everyone.

Even with the lack of sleep and nutrition, I possessed a phenomenal amount of both physical and mental energy. There was no stopping me at whatever it was that I wanted to do. I was going to do whatever I pleased and irritating me would bring nothing but severe repercussions.

During this first week of November, I had to attend school as usual, but I was there in body alone. My mind was caught up in daydreams which eventually blossomed into full blown delusions. I began daydreaming that famous people that I liked were actually my cousins. For example, many rock stars, movie stars and professional athletes were my cousins. It didn't matter what race color or creed they were, if I liked them, they were my cousin.

Needless to say, any kind of studying or attention to class was out of the question. I didn't need school anyway. I already knew everything through divine intervention. There was absolutely nothing anyone could say to me that would change my mind on this point. I firmly believed this manic delusion and I was elated. As in the intensity of the depression, I believe the intensity of this elation to be ten times greater than a normal specimen's elation. The thought of knowing everything was fantastic multiplied by ten. I don't care if it was based on reality, it was the greatest sensation I've ever known or probably ever will know and it was not drug induced. No drug could ever come close to this natural high. Unfortunately, I don't think I'll ever feel anything remotely like it, ever again.

The best part of the high lasted about five days and kicked in on Thursday, the first week of November. I like to think of it as the euphoria bomb because it was just that, a bomb that exploded inside of me and man it was euphoria the likes of which I had never known.

Thursday evening I borrowed my parent's car to go to the school gym. I knew that some of the boys would be in there playing ball. There was a three on three, half court game in progress but I didn't recognize any of the players. I asked them if I could play the next game, but they rudely ignored me. So, I picked up a ball, went down the other end of the court and put on a show as only a wild eyed manic boy could. I was moving fast, faster than fast. I was hitting every bomb and nailing every bizarre, creative lay up imaginable and I was elated by my performance and vocal about it accentuating every gem with a loud "ooooweee!" or "whoooyea!" Man was I excited, pumped behind my wildest imagination. After a while, I had successfully distracted everyone down the other end of the court. At first, I didn't notice them standing there staring at me, but when I did, I cockily yelled, "watch this!" I picked up the ball, ran down the lane, flew through the air, and almost slam dunked the ball. One of the guys down the other end shrieked in amazement, "Jesus Christ!" Jesus Christ was an apt description, but while he was at it he should've thrown in the old man himself, Buddha, Alla, the Pope, the apostles, a few saints, a couple of nice looking angels and mother Mary herself. Remember, I was only about 5'6" tall and suffer from a disease on the streets known as white man's disease. I couldn't jump. I was amazed at what I was able to do on this night. My adrenalin was enormous.

Following this grandiose display, the boys decided to leave the gym, not to go home, but to rouse me out. I didn't leave though, I shot beautiful bombs for about another ten minutes. When I did leave, they all went back inside and locked the doors behind them. They knew they were outclassed. More importantly, they knew I was acting strangely. Apparently, a strange, harmless sixteen year old kid is not allowed to shoot baskets by himself down the other end of the court in the gym of the school he attends. A school at which he is earning "straight A's." What does that tell you about society, sports fans?

I didn't go straight home, I drove around a while. I wanted to see how fast a Volaire station wagon could move. It moved pretty good.

When I went home I hit the stack of books that awaited me. I didn't do my homework, but I read my entire Chemistry book. Speed reading mania at its finest. That's right, I now knew everything about Chemistry and it only took me fifteen minutes. Whew. Anybody willing to stop me here for a reality check? Okay, I didn't get anything out of speed reading. I'm not a sponge, and I don't have a photographic memory. But, I did believe I absorbed everything I read.

Later that night, I listened, once again, to my favorite musicians, Neil Young and Jackson Browne. They were my cousins you know. Following this, I went to bed. I couldn't sleep.

I just layed in bed and deciphered all the mysteries of the world. I layed in bed the entire night and did not sleep at all. You see, when you have superior powers, you have to put in a little overtime. I was helping people solve their problems by sending out mental waves. Aren't I a great guy? On this night, I saved many starving Ethiopians by magically providing them food.

It's important I intervene at this juncture. These delusions were very real to me. They had replaced reality. Like I said earlier, nothing, with the possible exception of God's intervention could stop me from believing these thoughts.

The next day I don't remember vividly but I'm sure of one thing. Every woman looked good. I mean that in the most disgusting, vile way. After all, I was sixteen and I did have glands, multiply the lust by ten.

There was one notable girl named Donna Seznick. In my eyes, she was the most beautiful creature that ever existed. She was to be my one and only wife for all eternity. When I was to be batting for the Dodgers, she'd be in the bleachers ready to catch my home run blast. This was our destiny.

After our first period class together, I asked this beautiful girl out on a date. Normally, I would have been too nervous and shy to do this, but I was manic and had crazy courage. She politely said no, but my fixation with her was to remain. She was still the one destined to be my wife.

Following my being shot down by Donna, I managed to make it to all my classes despite the fact that my head, racing with delusions, started to continually tell me that I needed to be elsewhere. Where I wasn't sure. I remember sitting in class entertaining the delusion that I was actually in a conference room somewhere in the middle East bringing peace to that region. Of course, what I thought I was doing is what I was actually doing. I wasn't really sitting in a Huntington Beach high school, bored out of my gourd. I had a calling to save the earth and I was laboriously attacking this task while my butt and the rest of me sat perched in Algebra 2 Trig.

This particular Friday, although my memory is somewhat cloudy, I'm sure that I was giddy, woozy and a walking zombie all balled into one. I had no sleep for ages, but my body, I'm sure was ready to rock and roll at any given moment. This state of mind and body was very peculiar. The mind was very active solving world problems, while the body, dormant during classes, was ready and eager to play any contact sport. That's strange when you consider how exhausted I should have been and probably truly was.

Friday night was spent listening to my cousins' music. Let me give you a list of my cousins who performed for me that night via the turn table. You already know about my closest cousins Neil Young and Jackson Browne. Then, of course, there are all four of the Beatles; Jerry, Tom, Bob and Stu. Then there was every member of Supertramp despite the fact I didn't know their names. Who needs to know a cousin's name anyway. Let me not forget Bruce Springsteen, Bob Dylan, Tom Petty, Chrissy Hynde and Bob Seger. I think you pretty much get the picture. If I liked them, they were my cousin. Blood relatives from both sides of the family.

This night in bed was the same, I was too excited to sleep and too busy solving world problems. You wouldn't believe how much energy goes into solving those suckers. But, I was the guy for the job. I had all the energy and psychic powers.

Saturday morning, I vividly remember cleaning my room thoroughly. This alerted my mother to a certain extent.

"Archie?"

"Yes?"

"What's wrong with you?" she asked jestfully.

"Nothing," I paused. "I'm cleaning out this room."

"Yes, I see that. Now tell me what's wrong with you?"

My mother has a terrific sense of humor. She probably inherited it from her cousin, Henny Youngman.

Following my chores, I grabbed my baseball glove and ball, a basketball, a baseball bat and an apple (I had to eat something), got on my bike and headed for my friend Randy's house. He was glad to see me and we played catch with our mutual friend Roger. Roger spent most of his time trying to hit my "vorhees" curve ball. He wasn't a bad hitter, but he couldn't hit this pitch. I would throw it directly at him and it would break about eight and a half feet across the plate. He foul tipped one or two but that was all. I wasn't a pitcher but I was throwing a very good curve ball on that given day. I had learned to pitch like that from my cousin and good buddy, Tug McGraw, the feisty and colorful relief pitcher of the Philadelphia Phillies. He taught me well, nobody could hit my pitching.

The rest of the day was spent playing basketball and studying for an Algebra 2 Trig test that was coming up on Monday. I was flying like a kite with boundless energy and strength. Everything I did felt right and there was no reason for me feeling this way. It was just another Saturday night in the life of a sixteen year old all American boy. However, on this Saturday, I was a bundle of raw energy and everything I did, I did much better than I used to and I was truthfully no slouch to begin with. I had always been a decent all around athlete and I had always done well in school but all of a sudden, I was great at everything without trying!

Of course, my thinking was becoming estranged from reality, but who was to notice since my activities were all geared around action and I was keeping my supremacy a secret in fear of being immodest. Yes, I was saving the world, but no, it was not my place to say anything. So who was to notice? It was not uncommon for me to be active, that was my nature. What was uncommon was the fact that I no longer had the ability to stop. I hadn't slept in days, felt great and didn't tell a soul. I thought I had been chosen to save the earth and I was up to the task and at this point I let no one know my secret.

This was the most exciting time of my life and I had no idea why it was me to be called upon to save the earth. Oh yea, I almost forgot, it was my supremacy. This was my reality. Can you imagine what a high it is to actually believe in something like this? I do, I lived it. I would give anything to feel this way again as long as it were based on reality and there was no aftermath. It's actually a sad notion to think the best time of my life was firmly entrenched in insanity.

Sunday brought basketball, basketball, basketball. Saturday night had brought insomnia, insomnia, insomnia. Still, my tireless energy persisted as I motored around like a madman. My mind was wandering but my body was continually in motion. I suppose by Sunday I was the point of no return and well into what many would consider a serious nervous break down. There is such a grave social stigma towards those who have nervous breakdowns or display any kind of "crazy" behavior, that it took me a long time after the ordeal to admit that yes, I had a nervous breakdown. It's a hideous and unfair stigma that can only be understood when you cross the line and actually have a nervous breakdown. It is unfair because the person who breaks has absolutely no control of the situation and this is akin to somebody being born with a particular color of skin. Up until the point of the breakdown, it is probable that the person never thought of themselves as being "crazy." I hadn't. This made it extremely difficult to accept, and knowledge of what it was that caused the break is no help in accepting the facts.

After basketball brought hours of studying for my Algebra 2 Trig test. Okay, seven minutes went into studying—four to read the entire book, three for review. At that point, I knew everything about the subject, and if by chance I didn't know everything, divine intervention would see me through. After all, look at all the work I had been doing for the old man.

Following my study session I listened to music and played the guitar. I wasn't a great guitarist, but with my innate abilities, I figured I'd have the guitar mastered in a week. I'd be better than Hendrix and Clapton in no time. No sweat, babe.

Another sleepless night was to come and my delusions really began to mount. I was gone. The person I always knew myself to be was no longer present. I had become this little ball of confusion and I was now intensely immersed in this delusional world. I was hopeless and this Sunday night was the eve of the single most pivotal day of my life. I call it dark Monday.

Monday, November 10, 1980, found me springing out of bed and raring to go at 6:30 A.M. The alarm clock went off and I'd like to say that it awoke me, but it didn't for I was wide awake. I had spent another night caring tirelessly for the less fortunate types of the world. Somebody had to do it, and I was the chosen one. Not an ounce of sleep to prove my toil.

My first class was Algebra 2 Trig. I received my test and finished it in ten minutes. It took the rest of the class the entire class period to finish. What a pack of idiots, eh? While I was sitting there, bored out of my mind, I began whistling rather loudly and I wasn't even aware I was doing it. Mr. Goodbar, my teacher, became very irate, "alright, who's doing that whistling?" I waved to him with a big old smile on my face and he came to my desk in the back with a terse, "knock it off Archie and finish your test." How rude he was, so I had to tell him, "I already finished my test Mr. Goodbar." He was amazed, "already!?" He took it off my desk and said, "Well then just sit there and be quiet," he then walked back to his desk, shaking his head. With a smile the size of the cheshire cat's, I acquiesced to his request of being quiet but did not do so 100% willingly. I seriously entertained the notion of whipping out my harmonica and playing a few tunes. I thought better of this however, figuring it best to let the idiots screw up their tests in peace. I found out months later that I got a 40 out of 100 on the test. Do you believe that, me a supreme genius and all the studying that went into that test? Goodbar must have dropped some acid before grading my test. That idiot was wrong, but that's the grade I received.

The only other class I remember that day was Advanced Placement English. I remember this class for two reasons: one, Donna Seznick was in it and I kept visualizing her naked. And two, I kept playing the harmonica and kept getting away with it, too. Miss Bryant kept getting annoyed, "is someone playing the harmonica in here?" I kept hiding it away and doing it again until after about the tenth time she finally nailed me to the wall and politely told me to stop disrupting the class and pay attention. I agreed only because she was a sweetheart, and because it was time anyway to gawk at Donna and visualize her naked. It's hell being a sixteen year old boy.

The rest of my classes went by like a blur but during one of them, I became extremely elated because it suddenly dawned on me that all my great cousins were going to throw a party for me on this very night. There was no school tomorrow due to Veterans Day and it was an ideal time. It would be a coming out party for me and I would finally be recognized for all of the wonderful work I was doing while I should have been sleeping. I know it was supposed to be a secret but I am too smart to be fooled. As a matter of fact, I was surprised it had taken me so long to figure this out. Needless to say, I was struck by the euphoria bomb and brimming with exuberance that was barely containable. I wanted to run the hallways naked and sing with glee but I knew where I was and how important it was to keep myself in check. So, I rode out the remainder of my classes with the biggest most deranged grin I could possibly muster. I also tried to take naps in my classes with my head on my desk. I figured if I was going to be the guest of honor, I better get some serious rest. In one of my classes, Joanie, a friend of mine, asked me if I was alright and I looked up at her with that psycho grin of mine and answered, "you better know it baby," and went back to "sleep." She laughed nervously knowing full well that I was acting strange.

I couldn't sleep even in class, and we all know how boring high school is, but the day eventually came to a halt. My last class was over and it was party time! The first thing I did was go to my locker, pick up my books and baseball glove (I brought it along, you never know when a baseball game will break out), and then I headed straight for the gym to play some ball with my old teammates and buddies. One problem, they were a team and had practice. Fortunately, practice hadn't started yet. There was a bunch of them just shooting around and warming up. So, I jumped in there with vigor, grabbed a ball and started nailing everything in the thirty to forty foot range. I remember how light everything felt, as if I were walking on air. Everything I did, I did right. This feeling was phenomenal as I drilled every shot from every part of the court inside the half court line. My friend Danny who was feeding me the ball, shrieked, "Jesus Christ, Arch, it looks like you have your old confidence back!" It wasn't old confidence coming back, it was new confidence forging forward with enough might to break through a solid damn. There would be a new me and it all started on this day. My day! I doubt I'll ever be able to come close to capturing that extreme self confidence, but on November 10, 1980, I thought I would soar to heights higher than heaven.

Then, trouble struck. Coach Eugene R. McNally stepped out of his office. What an asshole. He saw me once the previous year. He looked me over, taking note of my tiny stature, and maliciously growled, "yea, well you better be good." He broke a fifteen year old boy's confidence without even giving him a chance. What an asshole. Let me say it once more so that you get the gist of how I feel about the man. What an asshole. Who would break the confidence of a fifteen year old boy for no apparent reason? I'll tell you who, Coach Eugene R. McNally. He's listed in a medical dictionary as "Assholis Maximus Filthius." I'm sure you get my point.

He was the new J.V. coach and a very good one I might add. But that's as far as I'll go in the way of compliments.

When he came out he gathered his players to start practice. I did not leave. I stayed with the boys. McNally looked at me as if I were so much shit on his shoe.

"You, in street clothes, out."

"No," I wasn't budging.

"What did you say?" the asshole has a hearing problem, too.

"I said no," I spoke calmly and succinctly so the idiot could understand me.

"I am only going to say this one more time. Get out!" His big, fat, ugly face was beet red.

"And I'm only going to say this one more time. No." I was in his face with this one, yet calm.

"Out!!" I think he meant business.

"No. My parents pay taxes that helped build this fucking gym and I'm a student at this school. I have as much right to be in this building as you do." I made sense.

However, McNally commandeered one of his big meathead forwards to "escort" me out of the gym. McNally knew he couldn't touch me, but one of his dunderhead boys could.

His name was Bud Guinness and he was at least 6'3" and weighed probably 210 lbs. He came at me like a truck, full force. "Get out Archie!" He pushed me. I pushed him back. Everyone was stunned at this, but there was no fear here and if they thought I was going to run, they had another thing coming. He pushed me again. I pushed him again. The others watched in awe. Half of them were my friends, but they were in no position to help me.

Eventually, after sharing loving pleasantries, we grabbed each others biceps and began to dance. I began to dance backward for a while, but suddenly the old adrenalin kicked in and he couldn't get me past midcourt. Wasn't he and the others surprised? Surprise! Surprise! They found out that size isn't always the common denominator to strength. We were at a standstill for quite a while, when I stuck my thumbs into his biceps. Boy, did his eyes bulge with pain. He was in pain and I'm sure he was frustrated by the fact that he couldn't kick a "whimp" like me out of the gym. I felt for his poor suffering ego as he screamed once more, "Archie! get out!" I started to think at this juncture. I had proven a strong point here. He was not going to get me out of the gym no matter how hard he tried. The others knew this as well. I had frustrated and exhausted him and I was fairly certain by this time that I could have beaten him up pretty handily. But I don't like to fight. Then, I thought, let's go play baseball.

"Alright!! Alright!! I will leave the gym!" Guinness and I let go of each other and man was he panting. I looked at him sternly and softly said to him, "You aren't so tough Guinness, don't you forget that," then I blew him a kiss and walked out of the gym.

I grabbed my baseball glove, which I left in the locker room before going into the gym. I marched abruptly to the baseball field without even knowing if anyone was out there. It was off season, but when I got out to the field, sure enough, there was a guy in left field shagging flies. Without saying a word or asking permission, I ran out to left field and started stealing pop flies off this guy. I would run right in front of this guy and make the play. I was amazed that he didn't say buzz off, because this sort of behavior in the baseball world is considered rude. As a matter of fact, this guy complimented me on every catch I made. Pretty soon, we were like old buddies just taking turns catching pop flies. Eventually, I moved to center and the guy hitting the ball started to nail me a couple. I was making good plays, but baseball began to do what baseball always does to me, it began to bore the snot out of me. My mind wanders when I play that game and on this particular occasion, my mind was gone before I had started. So, after twenty minutes of spectacular play, I thanked the fellas and went on the roam.

I started to head back toward the school and gym with my head full of how great my party was going to be. It was then that I noticed the drill team practicing their act for the upcoming basketball game. Oh, boy. Twenty-five beautiful girls banging out their act. This was a job for me. I walked right through their act as they saluted me and smiled at me. Baby. This salute was no doubt part of the act, but I thought they were actually saluting my greatness. Maybe they had heard about my supremacy. Nonetheless. I was having a great time entertaining the notion that I could have any of these girls I wanted. All I had to do was point at one and she'd come running up to me, put her arms around me and never let me go. Absolutely. I thought, well, let me see, Joanie Sucrast looks nice today, but she ain't no Donna Seznick. Donna Petrie's a babe in that pony tail, but she ain't no Donna Seznick. Debbie Lyle would be fun, but she ain't no Donna Seznick. Come to think of it, none of those beautiful creatures was Donna Seznick. So, I sighed and moved on wishing that every girl in the world was my bride to be Donna Seznick.

I got to the gym and decided to give old fathead McNally a piece of my mind. I decided to wait until practice was over. After all, I did have respect for the game, and a practice should not be interrupted. So, since I had to wait and was boiling over with energy, I decided to walk around for about a half hour or so. I walked around the entire campus poking my nose into everything, but wound up rummaging through the trash out by the trailers. My mind wasn't on the things I was looking at, it was on the party the greats were going to throw me. Man it was going to be great! I finally get to meet them all and they're all there to pay homage to me. Yes.

After a while I walked over to the locker room to wait for the king of sloth. I was there but five minutes when out of the gym came my boy. He was alone, and I got my chance to speak my mind. I ran up to him but he saw me and started yelling, "Get out of here you crazy little bastard!"

"No, you get out of here, you fat fucking slob!"

"I'm not even going to talk to you, you good for nothing punk!"

"I just wanted to say," I started poking at his massive gut, "I wouldn't play for you if you gave me a million dollars." I assumed this hurt him deeply, but all he said was, "good, I wouldn't have you on my team anyway!"

"Fuck you!!" I screamed in his face.

"Fuck you!!" he screamed back and abruptly disappeared around the corner. I didn't even get the chance to tell him I was going to buy him a mirror so he could see how fucking fat he was. Nevertheless, it was a major moral victory for me. I had finally spoken my mind to a man who had unfairly broken my confidence the year previous. Kids reading this, it is wrong to tell off teachers. Unless it's Coach Eugene R. McNally. Then by all means, wail away. Throw an "asshole" in for me.

Chapter Three

I rode home on my bike as fast as I could, anticipating the party that was going to be held for me. I wasn't thinking about McNally anymore, the following day was Veteran's Day and I wasn't going to see him anyway. All I was concerned with was the party. It was all consuming. It was supposed to be a surprise and, indeed, I had no idea where it was being held. It was my mission to find out that information, show up, and act surprised.

When I got home I saw my basketball sitting in the closet. How could I let such a beautiful thing go to waste? I had to go up the street to the elementary school and shoot a few baskets. The party would materialize later. I was sure of this.

A note: At this point in time, I had no ability to stop. This is a hallmark manic symptom. Perpetual motion is a great clue that mania is or will be present soon. In this case, I was long gone, out of control and possibly unstoppable. Other people did not notice because it happened so quickly and I never displayed any symptoms prior to this bout. At the time, I believed my delusions, was riding the euphoria and never thought of myself as mentally ill. When I get like this, and I have been half a dozen times later, I'm already too far gone to stop myself. Unfortunately, it's usually other people who have to stop me and on a few occasions those people were big, tough guys wearing blue uniforms and carrying guns. After many years of dealing with the disease, I know the symptoms but sometimes I can't stop them even with the medicine I take religiously. A symptom that is a dead give away is insomnia. If I can't get sleep for a couple of days, I know my ass is dead in the water and I'm in for a ride.

All of this aside, as I was shooting baskets, it occurred to me that the party might be somewhere in the neighborhood. I couldn't stop thinking of all the great gifts I was going to receive, so I tucked the ball under my arm and set out into the neighborhood to do a little investigating. If there was a party to be found, I'd find it.

As I started to roam the neighborhood, I remembered that Donna Seznick lived only three blocks from my house. Where else would the party be held than at the house of my lovely bride to be? I strolled casually with a big old psycho grin on my face. I remember actually feeling life and how utterly fantastic it was. There was no sense in rushing over there, the party would be there and I was to be the star of the show. Wow, what a life I had!

When I finally meandered over to Donna's street, I realized I had overlooked one thing. Her street was divided into two by a greenhouse. I wasn't sure which house was hers (I only knew what street she lived in by looking it up in the phone book). It did not dawn on me that there was another side to the street and that she might live there. There was only three houses on the side I was on, so my chances were pretty good. I was a ball of excitement and nerves when I knocked on the first door. An old man answered and I politely asked him, "Is Donna Seznick in?" He looked puzzled and informed me that there was no Donna Seznick living at the premises. Smiling, I asked him if he was sure. Smiling, he assured me he was sure. Strike one.

The second house I went to held the same anticipation for me but no one was home. It didn't dawn on me that there were no cars around. Still, I thought, this could be her house. Maybe I was early? Then, I was convinced that this was the right house. Absolutely.

But there was one more house to check just to be on the safe side. I went across the street and knocked on the door. As I waited for someone to answer the door, a firm delusion gripped me. The delusion was this; if I was 100% Irish, everyone was 100% Irish. This was a strange one that lasted quite a while. The door finally opened and a young Asian woman stood before me. I didn't say anything and just stood there, entertaining my new delusion. Obviously, this woman was not Irish looking, but indeed she was Irish. Strange. She stood there looking at me as if I were from Mars until I finally asked if Donna Seznick was there. She didn't appear to be able to understand me so I asked again slowly. In her thick accent she said, "no, no Donna leave here." I became very frustrated by her reply and rudely insisted that Donna must live there. She replied again that, "no, Donna leave here." Then I stupefied her, "isn't it great being Irish?" With a more than puzzled look on her face, she said, "I no, no Irish. I Korean." And with that, she took her puzzled Korean face inside and slammed the door on me. I was out of houses.

I dejectedly started walking home, trying to figure out what was up. I figured they were just hiding Donna for the festivities of the night. It also occurred to me that the party could be held somewhere else. The more I brooded, the more frustrated I became. In this manic state, as in the others I've experienced, when delusions don't pan out agitation becomes prominent.

At this juncture, I was frustrated and irritable as I walked dejectedly homeward. After all of the dreaming and waiting for this party, nothing had yet materialized. They were making me pay for my future greatness by frustrating the bejesus out of me. Yet, I was still certain that there would be a party.

As I walked along, I noticed Dina Gomez's house. She was a girl I knew from school. She was nice and very cute but she was no Donna Seznick. Still, the party might be at her house. So, I stepped back, turned around, walked up the walkway and knocked on her door. She answered the door with surprise (I didn't know her well), "Archie, what are you doing here?"

"Oh, I don't know," I said sheepishly as I shuffled my feet, "I thought that maybe somebody else might be here." I gave her a knowing look but she didn't seem to know. "What are you talking about?" What an actress! This girl was the perfect front woman. I laughed, "You know. About my party." She insisted on continuing her facade until I almost believed she was innocent. I persisted, "you know the party that's being held for me by my cousins."

She looked more befuddled than ever, "Your cousins?"

"Yea, you know, Jackson Browne and Neil Young."

She started to look genuinely concerned and amazed at once, "Jackson Browne and Neil Young are your cousins?"

"Well, to name a few," I was beginning to feel a little uneasy, thinking I had the wrong girl.

She, on the other hand, was starting to get a kick out of my story. Who could blame her, it sounded like a prelude to some bizarre joke. She looked at me with a game smile, "Who else are your cousins?"

"Well, let's see, there's Bob Dylan and Eric Clapton and the Philadelphia Phillies," I spoke softly, my eyes averted to the ground.

"The Philadelphia Phillies are your cousins!?" She began to howl with laughter and then she called up to her older brother to come down and hear my "story." When I heard her laugh at me I almost began to cry and abruptly headed out to the street. She ran out and caught up to me in front on the house next to hers. "Archie!! Don't go! I'm sorry I laughed." She convinced me to hang out on the street and talk a while. She was sincerely concerned and tried to get the whole story from me. She now knew I was not joking and earnestly believed what was coming out of my mouth. Her eyes softened and she spoke softly and sympathetically, "Archie? What do you mean the Philadelphia Phillies are your cousins?"

"Well, they're all Irish and they're my first cousins."

"But Archie, there are black men on the Phillies."

"Yes, but they are Irish, like you and me are Irish."

"Archie, I'm half Mexican and half Filipino." She seemed to be feeling a little sorry for me."

"No, you are Irish." I was insistent and she acquiesced.

"Okay Archie, I'm Irish." Of course she was just appeasing

me. "Now what about a party?"

"Well, they're throwing a party for me and Donna Seznick. We're getting married."

"What!?" She didn't believe me. "You and Donna Seznick, no way!?"

At this point Dina's older brother called out his bedroom window. "What's going on down there Dina?" Dina looked at me and then turned around and yelled up to her brother, "Hang on Fred." She looked at me again and said, "Hang on a second here, Archie, don't go away!" I waited a couple of minutes while she went into the house and told her brother the story. She then came running back to me looking very concerned. "Listen, Archie," she paused and appeared to be near tears, "there is something wrong with you and I think you should go home and talk to your parents." She was right and I thank her to this day for her concern. I turned in the direction of my house, planning to do as she advised. Then, I heard her brother scream out the window, "Is Sammy Hagar your cousin, too?" The bastard got a good laugh out of that. And then I thought about it, maybe Sammy Hagar was my cousin. I knew he was a rock star, come to think of it, yes, Sammy Hagar was my cousin. There was a spring to my step after this revelation. I started to walk home with pride.

My mind changed gears quickly and I did not heed Dina's advice. I made an about face and headed to Edwards Street, the street that paralleled our tract neighborhood. I was thinking about my new cousin, Sammy Hagar. Would he be at the party? Was he a good musician? Then, I thought, who cares? Donna Seznick was more important to think about and as I walked around the tract, my obsession for her grew to monumental proportions. Oh, how great it was going to be to live my life by her side.

Another thing that grew was my paramount anticipation for this party. I had to find it and fast. It was much like searching for a urinal when you've had to pee for two hours. The momentum of this feeling was becoming unmanageable and my enthusiasm was to the point where it almost literally overwhelmed me. There was only one more place in the neighborhood that it could be—my friend Hasseim's. I bounced my way over there wearing my psycho grin.

When I arrived at his house, it was getting dark and the lights to his house were out. This was it, they were all hiding, waiting for me to show up. It's then that I heard Hasseim's voice from his darkened doorway.

"Archie, how's it going?"

"What are you doing Hasseim?" I asked with my knowing psycho grin.

He came up to me and said, "I locked my keys inside the

house and nobody's home."

"Aw, c'mon Hasseim. I know you're hiding my party."

"What?" He looked confused, which came to him pretty naturally.

"C'mon, I know Eric Clapton's in there."

"What?" He looked befuddled.

"You don't have to act surprised, I know there's a party in there for me."

Hasseim was shaking his head, "I have no idea what you're talking about."

"You know my party's in there, you can stop playing coy," I paused, "you know damn well that Eric Clapton is in there with a white stratocaster for me." He looked at me as if I were from Pluto, but then he seemed to think that it was a possibility.

"Eric Clapton is in there, really?"

"Yes," I said, "maybe they didn't let you in on it and are using you as a decoy. That's why they locked you out." This made frightening sense and I think I started him believing in the prospect.

"Seriously?" his jaw was touching the ground. He was a very gullible guy. "Eric Clapton is in my house right now?"

"Yes," I said emphatically, "so are a lot of other greats!"

He then thought about it and switched on me. He no longer believed. But I was still certain. As I spoke to him, I stood atop a three foot wall that enclosed his yard. He said to me in all sincerity, "Do you believe in God?"

"Yes. If I didn't believe in God, would I be able to do this?" I dove off the wall, headfirst, into the concrete sidewalk. Of course I broke my fall with my hands, but it was, nonetheless, a stupid stunt. Hasseim was shaken up by this, "Archie! What's the matter with you? Are you nuts?" Me nuts, never.

"Aw, c'mon Hasseim, it's easy. Nothing so simple could ever hurt me. Here, I'll show you how to do it." I hurriedly jumped back on the wall and dove off again, headfirst. I got up with a big smile on my face. "See, it's simple."

"Archie, you're nuts! You could have split your head wide open!"

"Are you kidding? I'm indestructible!" I stood up, beat my chest and laughed like a madman. I honestly thought I was indestructible. I jumped off the wall once more to prove my point and would have continued but Hasseim begged me mercilessly to stop. I didn't want to upset his weak stomach, so I did, indeed, stop. He stared at me in awe for quite some time as if he were observing a being from a different galaxy. I laughed heartily at him as he continued to stare as if he were mesmerized. This was probably his first encounter with a manic in the manic state, so his behavior wasn't odd. At the time, I didn't think my behavior was odd either.

I walked right up to him, "Look, Hasseim, I'm gonna go home, get cleaned up, and come back for the party."

"But there is no party here." He was extremely frustrated and this time there was something in his voice that convinced me that what he was saying was true.

"So where is the party?"

"I don't know, but it's not here."

When you're manic answers come quickly. They're not always logical and definitely not thought out, but they're answers nonetheless. Unfortunately, the manic will believe these answers are best, no matter how bizarre they seem to others.

"I know the party is up Edwards."

"Up Edwards, are you sure?" Hasseim had the same goofy, befuddled look on his face that was wearing rather thin on me.

"Sure, I'm sure. That's where I'll go," I started running towards my home. I yelled back to him, "I'm sure somebody'll pick you up." As I ran like the wind I heard him yell, "don't take the car!"

I made it home in record time and ran in the front door, into the hallway to the keypost, swiped the keys to my mother's station wagon and stole her car. Simple.

I felt an extreme urgence to get to this party but I remembered Hasseim and went back to get him. I drove through that zig-zag neighborhood, tires screeching. I drove right up to Hasseim standing on the curb and opened the passenger door.

"Get in!" I shouted hurriedly.

"Where are you going?" Was his reply. What an idiot.

"I'm going to the party you idiot." Being as he was an idiot, he got in the car. He didn't last, though. When I screamed around the first bend, he begged me to let him out. So, I stopped and let the whimp out. I told him he was going to miss the greatest party of all time and he pleaded for me to go home. I raced off leaving that poor chump in my tracks.

While racing off, I briefly thought that he was staying behind because the party was actually at his house. I quickly dismissed this notion, however, simply because a party for me would never be held at such an idiot's house.

Alas, I was on the path to the party. I had wheels and man was I using them. Early up the main drag (Springdale) I made, perhaps, the most insane decision I've ever made in my life. I was driving about ninety miles an hour and was rapidly approaching a red light with one car in each lane. I slowed the car down to about sixty, split the cars and ran the light. I estimate the clearance between the cars to be less than a foot. Whew! I could have killed someone, including myself.

The journey had only commenced and I was lost. Or could I be lost since I had no destination in mind? Anyway, I was supposed to go up Edwards but was doing ninety on Springdale. I figured it didn't matter though, I was certain Springdale would provide the same result. I would still make it to the party. Of course, I had no idea where the party was but I would find it. I was destined to find it, the outcome was pre-ordained.

At one of the first intersections I pulled up next to a lady on my left. I honked my horn long and hard to get her attention. When she finally looked my way, I looked at her as if to say, "Hey! Look at me! Don't you recognize me? I'm the great Arch! Everyone knows me!" She turned her head and I became a touch irritated. How could she not know me? I hit the horn again—same result. Now I was pissed off and yelling out the window for her attention. How could this bitch not know me? This time, she turned and started screaming at me. I could not hear the words but I know I wouldn't have liked them, so I screamed back, "FUCK YOU!" On that note, the light turned green and I was gone like a bat out of hell.

While I was driving up Springdale, my mind was not on the road. My mind was visualizing Julius Erving, the great forward for the Philadelphia Seventy-Sixers. He was flying through the air and making a slam dunk. I threw a delusion on top of that visualization. I began to believe that he and my father were mates during the Vietnam War. They had saved each other's lives and were mates, indebted to each other for life. This was a delusion that was way off base for my father was in the Air Force during the Korean War not the Vietnam War. He was stateside the whole time and never saw combat action. As for Mr. Erving, I don't believe he was ever in the military. Nonetheless, everything I thought was real.

The Julius Erving delusion lasted quite a while as I roared down the road in that paneled station wagon. I couldn't wait to get to that party to meet Julius in person. This thought made me drive even faster than my already blistering pace. I was zigging, zagging, bobbing, weaving, anything to get past the car in front of me. And all of this to get to a party, the location of which, unbeknownst to me.

In retrospect, I'm amazed at how skillful, albeit wild, my driving was during the course of this night. Driving is an instinct true enough, but my mind was never on what I was doing. My mind was entrenched in my delusional network and the only thing that meant anything was winding up at my party, a party that never existed. Needless to say, I was beyond being lost yet still I firmly believed I'd make it to the party with a huge grin on my face. I was to prevail.

I drove further and further into neighborhoods, towns and cities that were foreign to me. I then figured out that the radio was to be my guide. Yes, the radio would guide me safely to the party. I took everything that was said on the radio as a signal to turn right here or left there or to move forward. All the time I was speeding as the anticipation began to boil to a feverish pitch. I was certain, the announcement would come giving me directions to the party.

I wound up in a neighborhood in God knows what city or town. I figured this was it. I pulled up one side street and parked. I looked at the house in front of me and figured it must be the house. I tried to compose myself. I noticed that I had been sweating and breathing heavily.

Emotionally speaking, this was pure, untainted excitement. I sat in the car about thirty feet from my destiny. My destiny was of course—greatness. The adrenalin pumping through my veins was enormous.

I stepped out of the car, ran up the steps and rang the doorbell. There didn't seem to be anyone home, but that was their rouse. I knew I had the right place, so I decided to wait out the storm. After all, destiny had brought me to this house and I knew everything, so therefore it must be the house. How's that for logic?

As I waited, I blared the radio to decibels that could kill a horse. I began dancing, wildly and shrieking with ecstasy on the sidewalk next to the car. When they played "Hungry Heart" by Bruce Springsteen, I began jumping on the hood of the car like some baboon at Lion Country Safari. Then, I began running full speed, directly at the car, jumped on the hood, then the roof and then flew off the back to the ground. I repeated this process for about twenty minutes or so, and believe you me, you cannot get any higher than I was at this moment in life. Reality be damned, this was the feeling every man, woman or child hopes to achieve once in a lifetime even if for only an instant. And here I was, without achieving anything to cause celebration, as high as anyone could ever be and without the assistance of any kind of drug. Baby! These were the most exciting moments of my life; the anticipation mounting, the adrenalin flowing, and the destiny of a king awaiting. It's impossible to buy a high like this.

After a while I grew bored, yet not tired, of this foolishness. So, I decided to go for a walk while I waited. The street came to a dead end. Apparently, one of California's infamous rivers lived there, or was supposed to live there if any water were to miraculously appear in the region. I spent several moments throwing rocks into this dead river and it was at this time I actually came to my senses for a few moments. I realized what I had done and how hopelessly lost I was. I decided it was time to find out exactly where I was and how to get home. However, as I began to walk back to the car, I heard a song by my close cousin, Jackson Browne. It was blasting on my mom's car radio (I had forgotten to turn it off). When I heard this, the delusion network flooded my mind once again and the party of one resumed. I started the same jumping pattern on the car and I wildly danced on the sidewalk.

The people living across the street took notice of my shenanigans and the head of the household (we'll call him Bobbo) came out of his house and started yelling things from a distance. I didn't hear a word he said until he got right out into the street.

"What are you doing?" yelled old Bobbo.

"None of your God damned business!" I shouted. This apparently pissed my good friend Bobbo off.

"I'm gonna call the cops on you." Whoa! Big threat! They'ed probably lead me right to the party.

"Go right ahead, I'm on public property and I'm not hurting anyone." The old fart then yelled at me.

"You're insane!!" He then stomped back across the street into his house. I continued my jumping act nearly splitting my head wide open every time I jumped off the back. A lesser athlete jumping that way probably would have cracked their melon.

After a while, a cute, blonde haired old lady came walking down the street with her dog in tow. I rushed up to her and immediately asked her if she knew who my father was. She had a British accent and sort of laughed her answer. I guess I was a funny, harmless yet thoroughly disturbing character much like many psychotic clowns. She laughed, yet moved away from me.

"I don't know who your father is." She might've sounded convincing to some.

"Come on, you've got to know him. He was in England during World War II."

She seemed befuddled and slightly disturbed but she sensed my nature was good and played along for a while with what she thought was a joke.

"No, I have no idea who your father was," she chuckled and seemed to be waiting for a punch line.

"He's Audie Murphy, tell me you don't know who Audie Murphy is?"

She kept walking her dog as I paced with her.

"No, I have no idea who Audie Murphy is." I was puzzled but had one card left to play.

"You and he had an affair during World War II, don't you remember?"

She seemed to realize no punch line was coming and became a bit unnerved.

"I was a little girl during World War II and I have no idea who this Audie Murphy is, now will you please leave me alone to walk my dog." She was a nice old lady so I acquiesced. I walked dejectedly back to the car thinking how terrible it was for an old lover of Audie Murphy's to forget who he was.

The police were waiting for me when I got back to my car. Old Bobbo wasn't bluffing after all—bless his precious one carat heart. I wasn't alarmed by the presence of the police because I figured it was all part of the game. I had to pass these tests to achieve my greatness and after I passed what I was supposed to pass, the police would take me to the party. Simple.

As I approached the car, a large, tough looking cop addressed me.

"Good evening, sir." Indeed, I was a sir to him.

"Good evening," I replied soberly, sanely.

"We've had some reports that there's been a young man jumping on his car and making a racket. You wouldn't know anything about this would you?"

NOTE: There is something about a police uniform that'll sober up the most wild of manics.

"No, officer, I have no idea what you're talking about. I myself, was just getting ready to leave."

"Good," he said skeptically, "but before you go, you wouldn't mind showing me your license and registration would you?"

"No, of course not." I reached in my back pocket, whipped out my license and then retrieved the registration from the car. I handed it to the police officer with a smile on my face. He looked at me sternly, "Wait here." He then went back to his car to check me out. Upon his return he said with a sigh, "I don't know what you've been doing out here but I strongly suggest you go home as soon as possible before you get into trouble."

On that note I was out of there like a bat out of hell. I sped through that neighborhood as only I could with the police on my tail. I made short order of those boys in only a few quick rights and lefts. I was free to pursue my party and I didn't care if the police were sent to help me find my way. I would find my own way! I had one problem. I was still lost. Thank God I had the radio to guide me.

Chapter Four

    Soon, I couldn't even rely on the radio, it only became distracting to me and I wound up turning the damn thing off. It was at this point that I realized that there was something seriously amiss. The lack of sleep and running around had finally taken its toll and all I could do was pray to God for guidance, but not even he could help me out of this jam. I was starting to break down and was hopelessly lost with only a handful of change and my wits to guide me. Scratch that, my wits were no longer aboard the vessel. I had reached and surpassed the point of no return. However, this did not stop me from continuing my search for the party.
    My driving became slow and overcautious as I steered aimlessly into the night with no directions whatsoever. I sporadically turned on the radio to lift my spirits and to see if any directions to the party were to leak out of it. No guidance came and my spirits were not to be lifted. This was it, the end of the line.
    While driving, I began to sob mercilessly. It became so bad I had to pull over. I pulled into a shopping mall parking lot. There were a lot of Mexican people roaming around, and although I have nothing against any color or creed, I was scared.
    No words can describe my stay in that parking lot but I'll try. A deluge of tears came falling down as a deep seeded hideous laughter lunged out of me. I was both laughing and crying at the same time and every other emotion I've ever known came along for the ride. It was as if my soul were being purged and whatever force that pulled these emotions out, pulled them out violently and simultaneously. I don't know how long this outpouring lasted, but I would venture a guess of about twenty to thirty minutes. All the while the radio blared in a not so nice neighborhood. I was screaming out to be robbed, mugged, molested or abused. Fortunately, I was not harmed or bothered.
    Despite this severe break, I still firmly believed there would be a grand party held in my honor. All my friends, cousins, family awaited my arrival. That's when it dawned on me that my parents would know where the party was. More succinctly, my mother would know because she had planned this out ahead of time and had been watching over me as I led my seemingly

normal life. They hid the information that I was to be the greatest of the greats until it was my time to shine. They also didn't want me to develop an abnormally large ego. I felt sorry for my mother, having to listen to these God-like creatures arguing as to what my fate might be. But here I was, sixteen years of age and I had figured out their schemes and my destiny. I devised many delusions to answer all the questions that poured into my head . . . who did what and why, etc . . . and all of my answers were genuinely logical and fit my scheme of thinking. I was composed now and ready to phone my parents. Actually, I was getting pissed off at them for making me do all this leg work.

There was a pay phone out on the street and I went over and dialed the number. This amazes me somewhat. How could I remember the number under such duress.

My mother answered the phone.

"Mom!"

"Archie!? Where are you?" She seemed to be relieved to hear from me and mad.

"That doesn't matter mom. Where's the party and why are you doing this to me?"

"Doing what to you, Archie?" She began to sob, as my stepfather Ken took the phone.

"Archie, where are you, son?"

"Pa, I can't find the party," I began crying.

"Tell me where you are and I'll come get you."

Bingo! That was it. They had to come get me to take me to the party. This was just a little game. I was never expected to find the party but I was expected to try.

"I don't know where I am." I was thoroughly confused and frustrated.

"Son, go to the corner and get the street names."

I put down the receiver and ran to the corner. I was at the corner of Washington and Whittier in the city of Whittier.

"I'm at Washington and Whittier."

"Okay, listen to me now son. Don't go anywhere. We'll be coming to get you. Lock yourself in the car and don't move."

I followed his orders. I locked myself in the car with the radio blasting. It was amazing, I could barely hear the radio. My senses were overloaded.

Shortly after I locked myself in the car, the merciless sobbing, laughing and purging started up. I suppose the closest I'll come to describing this sensation is to take your most painful experience, and your most joyous, multiply both by ten, and then blast them out of you at once. It was pretty powerful stuff. Nobody on hard drugs could feel what I felt naturally. Several people have told me about great drug trips. I laughed in their faces. They have no clue.

NOTE: Although I was still entertaining the fabulous delusions of grandeur, this outpouring of both positive and negative emotions at once, started me in believing that there was definitely something seriously wrong with me. Up until this point, it was all excitement and games but now, pain and frustration entered the picture along with a little thing known as reality. I'm fortunate to have caring parents to retrieve me. I'm fortunate to have remembered the phone number. I'm fortunate nobody bothered me on the forty-five minute wait.

My parents, upon arrival, were understandably confused. On the one hand, they were upset that I took off with their car without a mention. On the other hand, they were deeply concerned about me and more than a little shocked at the state I was in. In such a brief period of time, I had become a total wreck. The only answer they could come up with was that I was on drugs. Nobody believed that I voluntarily took drugs, but they feared somebody might have slipped me something like PCP.

My parents found me in a total state of despair and exhaustion. When Ken opened the door to my mother's car, I popped out wearing a white towel and carrying an umbrella. I danced (or better yet swooned) for a moment thinking the party was about to begin. The bad times were over, rock and roll. Conversely, my parents must have been thinking the bad times were just beginning and indeed they were. I must have been one pathetic sight to them. There I was, a total wreck, and it was their job to clean up the mess. I can only imagine how hard it was for them to see their son in this condition.

My stepfather took me in his car as my mother took home the station wagon. On the way home, very few words were spoken but I blared his car radio on a rock station. This is pretty much taboo with my enormous stepfather, but he let me do it because he feared if he upset me in any manner, I might jump out of the car. He was probably right.

I didn't even know I was blasting the radio. My senses were completely overloaded and I was exhausted from my breaking down. Still, my stepfather was wise for not doing anything because I could still lash out or do something bizarre. Normally, I would never try to strike him in any way, but in this case, who knows? I could have very easily gotten us into an accident.

The delusions persisted as I softly cried the whole forty-five minute trip home. This time, it was about Dr. Hunter S. Thompson, the gonzo journalist. He dedicated one of his books to his wife Sandy. I was wondering how they were doing and if they were going to be at my party. For some reason, I vividly pictured Sandy, and she was pregnant. I had never seen the woman before, but I'm sure the picture in my head was her.

When we arrived home, they immediately told me to go into the den and not to come out until I was told. I complied, I was too exhausted to put up a fight. I sat in a comfortable, rounded, orange chair. I sat for several minutes, thoroughly drained, but again, even in an exhausted state, I did not fall asleep. Sleep was simply impossible.

After about half an hour, they let me out of the den and sent me to my room. I'm not sure why they switched me. Maybe they felt I'd be more comfortable playing records in my room. Who knows? I do know one thing for certain that I didn't know about at the time—they were making arrangements to put me into a mental hospital. Of course, they didn't tell me anything about this, for if they had, I would have gone ballistic.

Anyway, as I waited in my room, listening to my music, my nineteen year old sister, Kim, came knocking on my door and peeped in at me. She is bright and perceptive, and I'm sure she picked up on every detail of the saga. She looked concerned as she poked her head through the door.

"Archie? Are you okay?" I had never seen her concerned about me like this.

"No!!!" I lashed out at her.

"What are you on?!" she asked startled.

I wasn't on drugs, so I had to quickly come up with an answer. In a flash, I came up with the answer that caused my problems. I had only been eating saltines for days. Yes, that was it! I violently spelled out the answer on my bedroom wall and shouted at my sister. "I'm on yeast!!! Y-E-A-S-T!!! Yeast!" This scared the hell out of her.

"God!!!" she shrieked and slammed the door on my approaching face. I was left alone with my delusions as I waited to be sentenced. What were they going to do with me?

They had but one alternative. They had to take me to a mental hospital. I know it was killing them, but they had no choice. I know, for certain, that this course of action was tearing my mother apart. She gets very emotional whenever anything major happens, and this was probably the single most serious thing that had happened to the family since my sledding accident that almost killed me when I was ten. My stepfather was also affected I'm sure. However, it was his role to be the strong, responsible hand. A role he always played very well.

So we went for a ride. Not just any ordinary ride. A quiet little ride. I thought we might be heading for the party. Then I thought no. Then I thought yes. Then I thought no. Either way, I had no idea where we were and everyone was dead silent. Kim was with my parents and I and she seemed to be crying along with my mother. I began to console Kim who was sitting next to me in the backseat.

"It'll be okay. It'll be okay." That was the extent of the entire conversation on that twenty-five minutes ride to hell.

Chapter Five

Upon arrival at the hospital, I was oblivious to where I was or why I was there. It was very late at night by this time and I was exhausted, but still had energy reserve left. For some odd reason, I have always had the ability to keep coming when the chips were down. In this manic state, that ability to energize was even greater. I had been perpetual motion for many days—why should anyone expect to calm down now? Yet calm is what I was when I walked into the hospital. No fights. No trouble.

During the last few minutes of the ride to the hospital, I noticed that I had started to entertain auditory hallucinations. I started to hear voices, mostly, I started to hear crowds cheering for me and me alone. It was as if my disciples were enthralled by my finally coming to them after the years and years of waiting for me to blossom into greatness. These voices and exuberant cheering were very real, I could hear them loud and clear and they fit in so nicely with my delusions of grandeur. Why would a God-like figure such as myself hear dogs barking in his head when he could have applause, jubilation, exuberance? These hallucinations were great.

NOTE: The victim of an auditory hallucination believes that the hallucination is real despite the situation or circumstance. The hallucination takes precedence. For example: if you were sitting in a room and started hearing a voice, that unreal voice would become your number one priority and you would believe it to be more authentic than what was really going on in the room.

Now, at this point in time, I wasn't having terrible delusions, but later they were to come in droves. I mention them now because arrival at the hospital marked the arrival of the hallucinations.

The delusions persisted while I awaited my evaluation at the admissions office. I was thinking that it would be great if Hunter Thompson were at my party. Maybe he could give me a tip or two about writing? Maybe I could give him a tip or two? Who knows? After all, my potential was unlimited, right?

As we waited, I flipped up the bill of my "Yosemite Sam" baseball cap and pretended I was Holden Caulfield. Like Holden, I liked screwing around a lot. I jumped in a wheelchair and started doing donuts in the lobby. My mother discovered me doing this and started yelling reprimands. I didn't pay any attention to her and kept on with my Tom Foolery until I decided to stop on my own. That shows how far gone I was. I never disobeyed my mother. It always made me feel guilty to do so. But in this state, I could surprise.

Finally, the door opened. It was my time to be evaluated. I have no idea of the name of the guy who evaluated me but I do remember telling, at length, the story of my party and my greatness. I'm sure he immediately marked me down as having delusions of grandeur. I'm also sure he realized that I was a very sick boy and needed to change my address to the hospital for a while. Maybe a long while.

I was unaware of why I had to see this guy, and come to think of it, I was unaware of where I was. At first, I thought the party might be there, but then I thought no way. Why would my party be held in a shithole?

The next step was the physical. I was still thinking about Hunter Thompson when my blood was drawn. I noticed that my blood came out in solid chunks. Enter visual hallucinations.

After the physical, I was taken to the Emergency Admittance Unit (EAU). This is where the nightmare began. Everything was peaches as compared to what was to happen on this ward.

For starters, the first thing I heard was a huge man shrieking. He was in one of those isolated rooms they had and he sounded like an extremely irate bear. That gave me an immediate headache and scared the bejeezus out of me and Kim. We looked at each other as if to say, "what the hell is this?" Unfortunately, this was it, and I still had no clue as to where I was. It sure in the hell wasn't a party honoring me. Maybe it was an assignment for me to help these people—another mission from God if you will.

My family was with me every step of the way and I'm sure they were taken aback by the whole procedure. It's not every day you admit your son/brother into a mental hospital. They stood by me, though.

Since it was so late at night (between 11:00 and 12:00), there weren't many patients roaming around the ward. Apparently they were all asleep except for the wonderful wailing bear who mercilessly continued to howl up a storm. Kim and I were told to wait in the office just inside the locked doors of the ward. We were supposed to wait for some guy named Peter to come talk to us. I guess Kim's job was to keep an eye on me. What harm could little old me do?

I was in the office babbling to Kim about the party—asking her questions, trying to pry info out of her—then it hit me like a ton of bricks. I was incarcerated! I completely snapped out. I wanted out of that fucking place like I've never wanted to be out of any other place in my entire life. Those big metal doors with the barbed wire glass on top would not be a factor. I was going to go right through those mothers and little sweet sister Kim was not going to stop me. I had a party to attend, damnit!

From about fifteen feet away I ran to the door and karate kicked the wired glass, upper portion—BANG! The foundation of the thick metal door shook feverishly. I ran back and did it a second time—BANG! The foundation shook a second time. All the while I was sizing up that door like a piece of meat, Kim kept pleading for me to stop. Mind you, she wasn't foolish enough to get in my way. One of the smartest people I've ever met, that girl. As for me, I was starting to have fun. A third time BANG! I thought the glass was going to give that time. I was laughing hysterically and having myself a good old time. Kimmy was getting very upset. "Archie, please . . . please . . . please . . . stop!" I had never seen my sister beg like that before. She looked pretty damn cute. One more time for good measure—BANG!

"Okay! Okay!" I smiled broadly and rejoined her in the office.

We were waiting for my parents to fill out the paper work as this guy Peter finally showed up. He asked for all my valuables and I complied not fully aware of what I was complying to. Why did he want all this stuff . . . wallet . . . keys . . . change . . . etc. It then dawned on me that I might be spending the night in that dump. Reality phased in there for a while. Then, old Pete asked for my belt. I thought that odd, since belts held pants up. Did these people want lunatics walking around with their pants to their knees?

Old Pete looked me square in the eye, "May I have your belt please?"

"Only if you give me yours big boy." I laughed heartily. I sometimes do that you know.

"I must have your belt, sir," he was stern, yet there was a trace of fear in his eye.

The yes-no thing went on for a while until I finally complied with this little speech. "Peter, I'm gonna give you this belt on the condition that I stay here only one night. I just need one good night's rest. Okay? . . . Deal?"

"I can't guarantee anything," he spoke rather softly.

I held my belt in my hand and spoke rather sharply to this man who was only trying to help me. "You know, you aren't any better than the fucking lunatics in here. As a matter of fact, you're lower than these people and are too stupid to realize that. And you're scared, too. I see it in your eyes." He, sitting, looked up at me, standing. "Say whatever you want," he seemed more frazzled but aloof at the same time. I don't know why I was harassing this guy because he seemed really cool and he was just doing his job. Maybe I was harassing him because it was me who

was afraid and I was just projecting my fear on him.
"You're scared," I persisted, "and I'm only staying here one night. I only need one good night's rest."
"Okay, one night," he said coolly. I gave him my belt.
My stepfather and a couple of other people came back at this moment, and all of a sudden I felt a little boxed in. I knew it was time for him and Kim to leave me and the thought of being stuck there with all of that screaming began to play heavily on my mind. I had been getting tired talking to Peter, but now the adrenalin kicked in again, and once again I was wide awake and energetic. No sleep for five days was not enough to wear me down, so why should I go down now? If I were to sleep, it would come with a fight and a truck load of Thorazine.
I became uneasy when I was told that my family was to leave. I have no idea where my mother was—maybe filling out papers. All I know is that I didn't see her and I started to have this overwhelming feeling that I'd never see her again. An extreme angst filled my chest—a tightness purveyed my being. I was ready to explode.
It was at this point I got into a little scuffle with a few choice, meaty, mental health workers. I was so emotionally charged about hearing that my family had to leave that I made a desperate, last ditch effort.
"No!! I'm not staying! You guys can't keep me here!" As I looked into their eyes, I knew they were determined to keep me there. It wasn't a fair fight—three meatheads against tired, tiny me. Yet once again, I was up to the task. I approached the big metal doors as the meatheads stood between me and what I perceived to be freedom (the doors were, of course, locked). I made a quick move to the left, trying to get around meathead #1. He grabbed my right wrist and tried to pull me close to his body but I wrenched myself free and threw a wicked elbow into his gut which doubled him over. Instantly, meathead #2 jumped on my back, trying to ride me to the ground. I carried this large dude on my back for several feet, until I finally wrestled myself free. Upon watching his fellow meatheads fall prey to a runt like me, meathead #3 tried a different tack. He tried calm talk. I ran around the corner of the hallway on the ward, gearing up for another battle with the meathead brigade. These guys were persistent and right on my tail. Meatheads #1 and 2 were both large guys over six feet tall and bulky. Meathead #3 was only about five feet ten. He didn't seem as willing to fight me as the other two even though he was bigger than me. He wanted to talk things out and he spoke to me while the other two closed in on me.
Battle #2 ensued and the results were the same, I wasn't to go down and I didn't care if the meatheads got hurt. Elbows, fists, anything to get out and I successfully escaped again to yet

another location on the ward with the meatheads on my heels.

Battle #3 started, but this time my stepfather, who still hadn't left, intervened. This was a bright move on his part because I had never contested him either verbally or physically. He was a very big man—standing six feet three inches and weighing two hundred and fifty pounds. The whole war with the meatheads could have been avoided had they let him talk sense to me. But they were the professionals, they knew what they were doing, right?

"Archie!" Ken shouted as all three of the meatheads tried to wrestle me to the ground.

"It's not a fucking game, Pa! It's not a fucking game!" I was screaming as loud as I had ever screamed and the wrestling was growing more and more intense.

"I know, son, I know." He sounded upset.

"It's not a fucking game!" I screamed again.

"I know, son," he paused, "just stop fighting, they are not trying to hurt you, they're trying to help."

On that note, I finally let go of the reins and three large men fell on top of me. I could not contest my stepfather. I had to put down my weapons.

Now that I had let go, I let out a scream, a scream that can only be described as primal. It originated at the bottom of my soul and shook the entire foundation of my being. The sound I made captured the essence of my tortured being. The pain, the frustration, the fatigue—all were present and accounted for in my soul scream that seemed to linger for decades but only lasted an instant in reality. I let the meatheads pick me up and carry me to a small, dark room in the back of the ward. When I was carried into the room, I began to struggle again, but this time, I could not jar myself free. They struggled to put me into leather restraints that were attached to each bedpost of a single bed. After a while, meatheads #1 and #2 triumphed. I was left alone in that dark room in restraints way too tight for each extremity.

I shook that bed and screamed for an eternity. I was thrashing so hard the bed was jumping up and slamming down with a violent bang. I tried to free myself from those damn restraints that cut off all my circulation. No luck. So, I tried to chew off the thick metal shackles that held the strap to my wrist. No luck. So, I screamed and thrashed about more violently than before, and I verbally assaulted the three meatheads with every vile, fucking curse word known to man. Fucking pigs!

After about fifteen minutes of this, a doctor came in, turned on the lights, pulled down my pants and gave me a shot of something geared to put my wild, cute little ass to sleep. I desperately pleaded the man to take off the restraints, and then when he didn't comply, I called him names worse than the worst names known to man, and then I began spitting at him. We laughed about this later, once he knew what a sweet kid I was, but at this juncture, we were mortal enemies and given the chance, I would have take a juicy swing at him. How dare he not loosen my restraints. Didn't he know who I was? I was the great Arch for Christ's sake. I didn't need sleep. I didn't need anything. Let me go.

I started to calm down about twenty minutes after the doctor left. Those whole twenty minutes were spent violently thrashing and screaming. It's amazing how strong the human body is and how much energy can be expended. I had been testing the limits in those days before the final curtain, but I'm mostly amazed at how much strength I had left this late in the game. As I thrashed, tears flowed from me like never before and I noticed I was drenched with sweat from head to toe.

Eventually, I started getting tired and wanted to sleep. Then, a revelation struck, I was afraid to go to sleep, thinking I'd never wake up. Still, I talked myself into trying to sleep. It was silly to think I was going to die. Wasn't it? Anyway, I was going to try but didn't think I'd be able in restraints. So I yelled as loud as I could for help.

"Hey! Could you guys loosen these! I can't sleep!" I was starting to fade as my face lowered to the bed. My strength held out of for the time being.

"Heyyyyy!! I can't fucking sleep, would you guys loosen these!? Please!!" Pause. Nothing.

"Please!!" I wasn't sure if they heard me, so I kept on begging for mercy. "Please!!! I can't sleep like this! I'll be good! I swear!" The pilot light was fading as I continued my pleas for another ten minutes. Finally, at long last, my head hit the bed and I was silent. I wasn't quite out when someone took mercy on me and took off my restraints.

Those moments before they loosened me up, while my head was on the bed, all I could think of was dying. I felt closer, and probably was much closer, to death than I ever had before. I felt closer to death than I had when I nearly did die when I ruptured my spleen in a sledding accident when I was ten. I don't know how many people have ever felt this close to death but I'm sure not many have. I was fortunate to wake up the next day.

Finally, at long last, I slept. Boy, did I sleep.

When I awoke, I didn't know where I was or even who I was. the ordeal I had just been through had been nothing like anything I had ever experienced. In the same day, I had my highest high and my lowest low. And as I sat on the edge of the bed in the little locked room, I noticed I still had energy. I then tried to recollect what happened the night before. It all came back to me which explained why my entire body was stiff. At this point, I think I started thinking clearly. I was still in a dangerous manic state, but sometimes a period of lucidity creeps

Chapter Six

That night, I slept on a couch in some sort of storage room. The EAU was only a way station for patients until they went to the ward on which they belonged. There is limited bed space and they had to leave a couple of beds open for anyone coming in during the middle of the night, like I had the night before. So, I slept on this old couch in this unkempt storage room. I was given another truckload of drugs to help me sleep and they did a handsome job. I slept very soundly at night. Little did I know at the time, I was going to be taking drugs everyday for the rest of my life.

When I awoke, I was visited by Santa Claus. In fact, it was Santa who woke me. He poked at my stomach until I came to. "Hi!" he spoke jovially, "my name is Santa Claus." I shot out of the bed as if I had spiders in my underwear. I headed straight to the door screaming, "Nurse!?"

"I know you find it hard to believe. Everybody does at first. But, I truly am Santa Claus." I sat stunned, looking at him as if he were from Mars. But, you know, he truly did look like Santa Claus. He was short, fat, gray hair, bushy gray beard, glasses. Nahhh! Couldn't be!

"Here, stay here, I'll prove it to you." He spoke slowly and methodically as if he'd been shot up with Thorazine. He then left the room as I waited. I thought maybe I should ditch the guy and roam the hallways. But then, I thought, I might run into Jesus or Moses. I wasn't prepared to meet heavyweight religious figures like those guys. So, I stayed in the room.

When Santa returned, he brought me a gift. It was a book wrapped in newspaper. This was one of the many times I asked myself, "What the hell am I doing here?" He looked at me proudly and smiled, "I brought you a gift."

"Thank you," I replied politely. He wasn't a bad old guy, just a little confused. I, on the other hand, was very uptight and uneasy. I didn't know how to deal with psychotics. Of course, I was psychotic myself, but up until that point in my young life, I had never really met a bona fide nut. I thanked him again and told him I'd cherish the gift. On that note, I was hoping he'd leave me alone. He didn't.

"Have you been a good boy this year?"

"Yes," I said shyly. "I'm getting straight A's."

"Well then, it's a good thing I got you this gift. You're a very nice boy."

Of course, the man didn't know me and was unable to discern whether or not I was a good boy. But, when a pleasant, old, psychotic man thinking he's Santa Claus says something nice to you, you sort of just take the compliment. You know what I mean? I still wished he would leave me alone, but in a strange way I sort of liked the old nut. I mean, it was really nice that he chose Santa Claus as his psychosis rather than someone mean like Adolph Hitler.

I started calming down and actually began to enjoy the old man talking about reindeer. After a short while though, he just walked out of the room.

I sat on the couch a little befuddled and started to let my imagination run. What if he really was Santa Claus? Wouldn't it be truly like this society to put the real Santa Claus in a mental hospital? What about Jesus? Everyone is talking about the second coming of Christ and there have been many, many people who say they are that wind up in an insane asylum. What if one of those Jesus' were the real thing? Say Jesus comes back with no powers and all he wants to do is walk in the park and eat a hot dog and go back to heaven. He says to someone, "Hi! I'm Jesus Christ, how are you?" Wham! Slam him in the mental hospital. Nice way to treat the son of God. So, maybe this old dude was really Santa. Maybe his reindeer broke down in Anaheim and all he was doing was asking for help and foolishly let out his identity. Whamo! Straight to the twinky farm. Nice society. After letting the imagination run, I decided, what the hell, if the old guy wants to be Santa, let him be Santa. Who am I to judge? Who are you to judge?

After pondering this subject, the frustration in my life suddenly came to a boil. I started balling my eyes out for no apparent reason. Violent tears wrought with fears. I sat on that couch with my hands on my face crying tears of frustration and exhaustion. I did this for about fifteen minutes until Santa Claus returned. He came in hurriedly and grabbed my hand.

"What's wrong?" he asked as I were an upset child. I wiped my face as I looked at him.

"I don't know," was my honest reply.

"Didn't you like the present I gave you?"

"Yea. Sure I liked it," I noticed that he looked like he was going to cry as well. I reassured him, "Yes, it was very nice. Thank you Santa." He looked a little upset to me.

"I'll be alright, Santa," I tried to console him.

"I'll be alright too, as long as you're alright." Nuts or not, this was one hell of a nice man. He smiled at me and said, "I can see that you need to be left alone, so I'll leave you now," he left.

That was the last I ever saw of the man. I didn't seem him on the ward the rest of the day. Again, maybe he was who he said he was and was only giving me the gift of friendship when I needed it most. Nahhh!

Finally, after feeling sorry for myself for quite some time, I got up off the couch and began roaming the ward once again. I was lucid, and what I saw on that ward was quite a pathetic sight. Ten to fifteen grown adults broken and distorted. I felt sorry for them—sorrier for them than any group of people I've ever felt sorry for. Although I was as sick as any of these people, there was no way I was going to put myself in their category. They were wretched and haggard and all of the life had been taken from them. I, on the other hand, was young and full of energy and was chosen to be the greatest of the greats. I was being tested again. My job was to bring life back to these people. How? I don't know, for these people seemed beyond redemption.

After roaming the halls a while, a mental health worker stopped me and told me there was a doctor waiting to see me. She was an attractive, pregnant Mexican woman named Bertha Chavez. She had come to set me straight on a few things. First off, she explained to me where I was.

"Do you know why you're here Archie?"

"No," was my honest answer.

"Well, you're here because you need a rest," she spoke softly and politely.

"What do you mean? I'm fine," I honestly thought I was, indeed fine.

"Well, you've been a little erratic lately and we want to keep you here for a while to run some tests and see if there is something we can do for you. Would that be okay?"

"Yea. I guess so, but I don't like it here."

"Well we're going to move you up to the adolescent ward so that you can be with people your own age."

"When will that be?" I asked a little nervous.

"Either later today or first thing in the morning."

I wasn't sure I wanted to stay in the hospital any length of time, but the adolescent ward sounded like a better place to be. At least I didn't have to worry about running into legendary figures like Santa Claus or the Easter Bunny.

"Okay." I said, "I'll go to the adolescent ward, but I'm not staying long. I've got shit to do, you know?"

"Okay, great!" Bertha smiled. "We'll move you soon." On that note she left. My brief stay in the hospital turned out to be two full months and three weeks. I found out later, the doctors estimated my stay to be four months. What a fast healer I am! Oh boy!

That night, I was moved upstairs to the third floor—the adolescent ward. The best way to describe this ward is with three letters—ZOO! Put on your tank tops, grab your sun visors, buy yourself some peanuts for the animals—you have just entered a zoo. A zoo brimming with glands and adolescent energy. Be sure not to get too close to the animals or they might try to mount you. Yes, there were problems and more adolescent energy on that small ward than any single place I've ever known. Being the new kid on the block, it was my job to make friends as fast as possible. Normally, it takes me awhile to make friends, but in the manic state I was bolder and much more gregarious than usual. I met a girl right off the bat and we became immediate friends. Her name was Linn Sue and she was a beautiful Chinese girl. I usually have difficulty approaching beautiful girls in fear that they might spit at me, but in this state, I could do anything. Besides, Linn Sue was one of the coolest people I ever met and there wasn't much of a chance of her spitting on me for no apparent reason. There was an old pool table on the ward and she and I shot a few games together.

Note: I wasn't a very good pool shooter, but in the manic state, I could do no wrong. I held the table for eleven games beating every kid that tried me. It's amazing, when you're in a manic state, you can do everything better. At least, that's what you think.

I met all the kids on the ward while holding the table and I'll get to them at length later. What was going on at the table was far more interesting. I was doing so well, I became very cocky. As I mentioned earlier, the table was pretty old, and I was shooting with all of my strength and blowing the pockets right out onto the floor. This impressed the hell out of Linn Sue who laughed and smiled every time a pocket hit the floor.

After the eleven games with the other kids, I offered to show them my curve ball. I proudly boasted that the pitch broke eight and a half feet (it was more like six and a half feet). I sent Linn Sue down the hallway to catch for me. She was excited and smiled a broad white smile as she crouched to catch my pitch. The other kids looked on skeptically. I was just starting into my windup when I heard a very loud, feminine, "Stop!" It came from Esther, an elderly mental health worker who saw me through the window of the office. I loudly asked, "Why?" and she loudly returned with, "There will be no throwing pool balls on this ward!" I didn't listen as I went into my windup again. "If you throw that pool ball, you'll be put in restraints," she spoke sternly and assertively. In retrospect, I should have thrown the damn thing because I wound up in restraints. I wound up in them because I wouldn't put down the ball when I was asked. I stood there and taunted Esther by threatening to throw the old three ball. She picked up the phone and called for support. The support was three or four big ass brawny guys who could break me in half on their own, but, again, in this state I put up one

Bored out of my mind and my head was fired up like a rocket. Racing thoughts, the cornerstone of my problem, filled my head the whole time I waited to be released. The best way I can describe these thoughts is to liken them to that of a deluge. They came in rapid succession but they all came from different sources. There was no logic to their succession. One would be about one subject, the next, another subject. Yet, all of these subjects were urgent, real and important. And there was no way I could stop or even slow these wild ideas. It was magical in a sense. I had no idea my brain could work so quickly, but because it was working so quickly, it made it impossible to focus on any one particular thought. It was as if everything I had ever learned in my life was spilling out at once without me having a chance to think about one issue.

Eventually the ideas did slow down on their own and I was able to focus on the most important issue of the day—my party. I couldn't wait, particularly now that I'd paid some rather heavy dues. I deserved to be considered a great amongst the rock stars, athletes, writers and statesmen. Man, it was going to be great! I would be the guest of honor and all my famous cousins would be smiling at me aplenty. It was as if I were the tiniest piece of the puzzle that only needed to be gently fit into place. The trouble for the others had been finding me and putting me into place.

When I finally found my place, then peace would fill me and I would be at one with the universe. Everyone would be at one with the universe. Can you imagine that? Peace in everyone, found forever. A calmness and relaxation for eternity. Serenity if you will. All of it found for everyone. All that had to be done was find the tiniest piece of the puzzle and pop it into place. The Archie boy was that tiny little piece.

Chapter Seven

After a while of entertaining the most spectacular delusion less far, I became very restless and painfully aware of my confinement. Despite the amount of energy I had expended over the past week or so, I was still bouncing off of walls and there seemed to be no end in sight. I've mentioned this abundance of energy on several occasions earlier and probably will again, simply because it was so amazing. Confined to that little depressing room only enhanced the enormous energy level and being pent up made me furious. However, I was starting to learn the system, and I realized that acting out was not the way out the door. After all, they were professionals and they hadn't forgotten about me. So my tack was to simply be quiet and patient. Don't raise too much hell.

Still, with all that energy and confinement, I had to do something both physically and mentally to keep from exploding. But there was nothing to do. Or was there? I noticed a cardboard cup lying on the floor. It was empty and I picked it up and crushed it into a ball. It made a great baseball and there was enough room in the room to run around the bed—a perfect baseball diamond if ever I'd seen one. I stood at the end of the bed at the end of the room and started my game.

I'd throw the cup up in the air and hit it with both clenched fists and then I would run around the bed. the bases were the four bedposts. I had to touch all four for a homerun, three for a triple, two for a double and one for a single. I had to touch the bedposts before the cup hit the ground and if the cup hit any part of the bed it was an out. There were a lot of singles in this game. Indeed, I played a whole game running around the room like a lunatic. It was innocent enough though. I was bored mindless and just blowing off some steam.

Delusions came to me while I was playing the game. One of my favorite baseball players was Fred Lynne of the Boston Red Sox and he was in the game and immediately added to my list of all star cousins. He went four for four in this game and I'd be able to congratulate him myself at my party. Another person in the game who would be at my party was my genuine cousin Michael who somehow snuck into my delusional network and wound up hitting four for four in my little game. I saw him as an up and coming star for the Boston Red Sox. I sort of knew Mike wasn't a Boston Red Sock, but it fit into the scenario of the delusion.

Note: It's interesting to point out that I did not believe that everything I thought was real. Some things I knew were the ludicrous imaginings of a legendary day dreamer. What's truly interesting is which crazy day dreams became bedrock reality. There was no rhyme or reason to this selection whatsoever.

After playing an entire nine inning game, I was pretty tired from running around the room. There was nothing to do but lie down and wait. It was a terrible restless wait and I couldn't stop my head. I felt very much like a caged animal and I was mounting doubts as to whether anyone would unlock that damned door. I noticed the other kids walking by and peeping in the window of the door. They were laughing and joking at me and all the while, I felt lower than I had ever felt in my life. But one single thought came out of nowhere to lift my soul—I, and not them, was the tiniest piece of the puzzle that would bring harmony to the masses of the world. How could their snide, trite laughter hurt me?

Finally, at the end of the day, Cliff let me out of my cage. Cliff was a great guy who took good care of me and showed me to my room. Strangely, I thought Cliff was Jimi Hendrix. I didn't take into account that Jimi Hendrix was dead. All the time I was high as a kite, I kept expecting old Cliff to jump on a table and sing "Purple Haze" to me. Very funny. Later on in my little journey, I told Cliff that I honestly thought he was the actual Jimi Hendrix. The man thought I was hysterical. He literally fell down on the ground laughing and damn near peed his pants.

My room was a double room at the end of the corridor by the pool table. I had no roommate which was nice. I needed plenty of privacy for entertaining my delusions. Any kind of distraction would only complicate matters and hinder my ability to carry out my task of saving the world. I had to sleep alone if I were to magically solve the enormous problems the world confronted. Needless to say, I was relieved that I had no roommate. When Cliff was done showing me to my room, he left me to do as I wished. I played pool.

Due to being in the manic state, my pool shooting, as you can probably guess, was very aggressive. I was shooting well and kept blowing the pockets off the table. This sort of thing is not good in front of the office with windows. It looked as if I needed to be tied up again and that was the last thing I wanted. My wrists and ankles were still extremely sore from the night before. Nonetheless, I continued to play aggressively. I knocked a few balls off the table and one of them rolled and slammed into the base of the wall to the office. Some lady (Judy) came out and scolded me, "one more time and you get an infraction," she then stormed back into the office.

I thought to myself, "what the hell is an infraction? and who the hell is she to be speaking like that to a superior like me?" It turned out that an infraction was like a demerit. If you got a lot of them some form of punitive action was taken. You couldn't get weekend passes and go home to your family if you had such and such amount of infractions. I'm proud of the fact that in the first week of my stay, I had broken the North American record for infractions.

The nurse in the office who had come out and reprimanded me, along with anybody else on the staff, could give infractions. There were infractions for everything—inappropriate behavior in general, inappropriate language, inappropriate touching, inappropriate farting, etc . . . etc. It was so easy to see your name on that infraction board and the kids with their feet out the door forever were the ones who weren't on that board and hadn't been for quite some time. In the beginning, I had no idea what the hell was going on and the other kids kept telling me it was a good thing to see your name on the board. Bastards (oops! I just earned myself an infraction).

Anyway, the nurse who scolded me, Judy, was having a real bad day. I found this out by wailing another pool ball against the office wall. She came out hopping mad and informed me that, indeed, I had earned myself an infraction. I thought, "cool, what's an infraction?" She went back to the office and fortunately I didn't knock anymore pool balls off the table. I was allowed to play if I didn't nail any pool balls off the table.

After a short while of superlative play and daydreaming that I could wipe the floor with Willie Mosconi, the great pool shark, one of the kids came down the hall and approached me. Apparently he had just come from therapy or something. He approached me with a very aggressive, "who the hell are you?" I replied aggressively, "Archie McRae, who the hell are you?" He came back with an aggressive, "Tony Combiati." We stared each other down for a while. Why he was staring at me cockily, I do not know. Why I was staring at him cockily, I do know. In the manic state, if someone comes off the wrong way or is cocky, the manic becomes irritable and sometimes downright hostile. I didn't like the looks of this guy. He was bulky, about my height, and was made up of about 95% hair, all of it black. Another thing I didn't like was the way he approached me. He could have used a much more tactful approach. But no, he had to be a jerk and I had to gear up to trash him. I was waiting for him to make the first move because I have never started a fight in my life. Just as he was about to make his move, Linn Sue the wonder girl came bouncing down the hallway. She saved old Tony's ass.

"Hi guys! Are you playing?" She looked at the pool table. Old Tony grabbed a stick and said all tough like, "yea, we're playing." Linn Sue asked if she could watch. I politely said, "of course." She was a cool girl and I was about to impress her by whipping the pants off Tony the tough guy. I beat him soundly, knocking a few pockets off the table in the process. Linn Sue was obviously impressed. She kept staring at me and smiling at me with my every move. We were already buddies and I felt relieved to have already met a friend on the ward. The first friend is always the toughest to make and I had already found her. As for Tony, after losing pitifully, he said something snide and stormed off. Good riddance.

Linn Sue and I shot some pool together and really got to know one another. She was in for some wild psychotic trip induced by drugs. She claimed to have been extremely crazy and had to be put in restraints three times herself. I thought, "cool, a match made in heaven. we both had psychotic breaks. I'm good looking. She's good looking. I've been in restraints a couple of times. She's been in restraints a couple of times. We're perfect for each other." But then I thought of Donna, my wife to be. The idea of me and Linn Sue went right out the window. There was no way I could ever cheat on my one and only. Nonetheless, Linn Sue would become my closest friend and confidant. However, every time I looked at that girl, I wanted to throw her on one of those many couches and kiss her until her face exploded. Normally, I'm very shy about meeting and interacting with beautiful girls, but Linn Sue and I had a lot in common and we were in an environment that held no secrets. What I saw in Linn Sue I liked a lot. We had a silent romance the entirety of our brief relationship. I'd give a lot just to hear how she's doing today. I fervently hope and even pray that she has everything in life she desires.

That day, at the pool table, we were each to find a soulmate for life. Not only were we friends, we were allies in the war of horrors and uncertainty that is associated with being in a mental hospital. And that strong tie would not last our brief relationship but a lifetime. We are still allies fighting our memories and the stigma that our society foists upon the mentally ill. I'm glad she's my ally and now that I'm thinking of her, I realize what a strong ally she is. She's out there making her mark—I can feel it! That thought is more than reassuring.

Eventually the whole crowd made its way back to the living room and the pool table area. There were thirteen of us all tolled and each of us had our own unique, traumatic problems. Some were heavily into drugs and alcohol, others had behavioral problems in general, still others suffered from some form of psychosis. All of us shared one thing in common—we hated the idea of being mental patients. Some of us bonded well together, others despised the other kids. It was like being a part of some kind of sick sociological experiment—"yea, let's throw all these whacked out kids in a cage and see what happens. Maybe the mick nut will hit it off with the fruit loop Chinese broad." I, myself, found the way the relationships developed very interesting.

The body ratio was nine boys to four girls. I found it very interesting that there were both boys and girls. At the age we were, our hormones were bouncing off the walls. Still, at night, we all walked around in pajamas and bathrobes. I guarantee, looking at Linn Sue in a bathrobe was a treat I did not deserve. Of course, I remained a gentleman at all times, but my heart skipped a beat when I saw her that first night. I, being new to the program, had no pajamas and bathrobe and was wearing the same clothes I had been for about five days. Quite disgusting! The same old brown corduroys, the white baseball shirt with green sleeves and old sneakers with holes in them. Also, I don't remember the last time I had showered—maybe 1977.

Chapter Eight

At dinner, I sat with Linn Sue and Julie, Linn Sue's best friend and roommate. We ate in the school room at the end of the ward. The room had five or six round tables and everyone seemed to be eating with their friends. On that first night, everyone seemed to want to know everything about me. They also took the liberty of nailing me with quick witty jabs to see if I could take a punch and to see if I was going to fit into the scheme of things. I passed the test with most of the crowd, but there were the malcontents like Tony who refused to like me no matter how friendly, charming and witty I portrayed myself. I portrayed myself as I truly was—a straight "A" student with the lost of all sports, particularly basketball, and an unquenchable thirst for rock and roll music. This went over well and I decided to leave out the part about my superiority, my cousins, my party, etc . . . Those were my secrets and there was no sense in letting the little people in on them just yet. Besides, I'm a modest man and bragging about how great I am would not be in good taste and would only make the little ones feel small.

I had the opportunity to get to know Julie. She was a very tall, attractive, big boned girl with auburn hair and pretty brown eyes. We didn't really talk about serious matters, but I could tell she was a very cool girl. She was the type of girl who was fun and intelligent—someone you hang out with. She was going out with Craig, the football line man from Fountain Valley who was sitting at the table to our right.

Something very interesting about her going out with Craig. I rapidly discovered that there was a lot of romances going on in the hospital. There were many in the course of my stay. The only reason I could figure, other than the obvious reasons, was that being in a mental hospital is a very lonely and depressing trip. There is a constant yearning to reach out and become intimate with someone. Also, there are painfully obvious reasons why these romances occur. You put boys and girls with overwhelming hormones in the same locked ward, something is bound to happen. Kids will have a tendency to pair off and screw around while the authorities backs are turned. I myself, paired up with a beautiful little blonde named Maureen who was admitted a month before I was discharged. Of course, there was no sexual intercourse in most of these relationships. There was a couple who bragged about it after they took a half hour pass around the grounds together. They said they did it in the bushes over by the freeway. I doubt it.

Before I go any further, I'd like to introduce the cast of characters I lived with and bonded with. First the boys:

CRAIG—The defensive end from Fountain Valley High School who was involved with Julie. He was in for doing a lot of downers. He used to play on them.

JAKE—Mr. Cool long haired dude that beat up his mother and sister. He actually was kind of cool and I was surprised to hear that story.

DONNY—Very nice guy who was busted for possession of a large quantity of marijuana. He also snapped out entirely when the police came to get him.

BOBBY—Donny's buddy who drove me insane, and more insane, with his incessant, pathetic whistling. I have no idea what he was in for nor do I care.

RICH—In for chronic schizophrenia. Rich was probably the sickest of us all. He had been hospitalized three previous times and he was only sixteen. His life was unfortunate because he was bright and fun to be around when he was in his normal phase.

DAVE—He was diabetic and the ultimate party animal—dope and alcohol. He was basically nice and funny, but he was also the portrait of a delinquent.

TONY—SHITHEAD.

ROGER—The coolest dude alive. He used to play "Stairway to Heaven" on his guitar and taught me a few chords I didn't know. Again, in for drugs.

ARCHIE—In for being the greatest human being on the planet with many super powers. In reality, a severely affected manic depressive. Probably the second sickest member of the tribe (speaking from an organic stand point).

Now for the girls:

LINN SUE—Charming, pretty, intelligent, sweet, lovable buddy of mine. In for psychotic break induced by drugs. Co-holder (with me) of the record for being put in restraints—three.

JULIE—In for drugs . . . quite possibly the most mature and sane of our happy little family.

CHANG LE—In for organic psychosis of some sort (probably schizophrenia). She did not speak a word of English but I understood her very well one night at the dinner table when she reached down and grabbed my crotch while I was eating. Some would be flattered but she wasn't my type of girl. Without doubt, the second craziest member of the health spa next to Rich.

STACY—A diabetic who was painfully cheery at all times. I never knew why she was in this crew . . . maybe she was so nice all the time that people were taken aback by this.

All these descriptions are brief and flippantly phrased but rest well assured, each and every one of us were in for reasons that were threatening to our lives as we knew them. We simply could not handle the rigors of life on our own at that particular juncture of our lives. We were there to recoup and reassess. We needed time to get our heads together before we could face the real world again. It was a brutal trip for all of us at such a tender age, but it was essential that we be where we were. My guess and hope is that we all made the grade. I think it would hurt me deeply to find out that one of us didn't make it. I hope they are all happy, and healthy, both mentally and physically—including Tony.

That night, after everyone had gone to bed, I sat in my room, looking out the window, thinking of how great my party was going to be. They were holding me in this hospital so that they could gather together all of my heroes at once. They were going to get Donna ready to be married. Yes indeed, being in this mental hospital was just a mere pit stop and test of my character and courage. I would surely pass and walk as a free, triumphant and jubilant young man at a party for me.

I lied down in bed and tried to get some sleep but I couldn't because the building across the compound had some form of generator that made a lot of noise. It didn't make the noise all the time but wouldn't you know it, when I put my head down on the pillow the damn thing started blasting. At this time my hallucinations, both visual and auditory, took hold of me.

I heard a lot of people calling up to me from the compound outside, but when I looked out the window, nobody was there. I thought that very odd as I went back to bed. A short time passed and I heard the voices again. This time, I could've sworn I saw one person running behind a tree. I thought to myself, "What the hell is going on out there?" Then it dawned on me, these were people who were trying to attend or crash my party. Somehow they knew about it and were privy to my whereabouts. This sort of scared me. There are a lot of lunatics out there looking for a great person like me.

I went back to bed a little concerned. Again, I was not able to sleep. The noise of the generator and the thought of those lunatics running around kept me from resting.

NOTE: A distraction like a loud generator, or even soft music, will keep a person in the manic state from sleeping because a manic is very easily distracted. Of course, visual and auditory hallucinations don't help matters any. No matter, the point is that I couldn't sleep again and the hallucinations began to drive me up the wall.

I heard people calling three floors up to me. They all ran behind trees and hid when I came to the window. I frustratedly went back to bed, but every time my head hit the pillow the voices called out to me again. Again, I went to the window and again nobody surfaced. Around the third time this happened I caught a glimpse of them running behind a tree. I began to scream at the top of my lungs, "Who are you?!!! . . . what do you want?!!!"

I yelled all sorts of things at these people and nobody materialized. I was going absolutely berserk over this and I expended a lot of energy shouting at these intruders. Of course, they did not exist but I genuinely thought they were there. Again, this was my reality and nothing could change my mind. I was dead certain there were people running around outside yelling my name and I was in a manic frenzy screaming all sorts of things including, "where's the party?!!!" I had to find out where my party was and fast or I'd go completely insane. Little did I know at the time, but I was already completely insane.

I yelled for about five minutes until Glen, the night shift worker, came in to calm me down. He was a very large black man with a very caring voice, "what's wrong buddy?" I was frightened as I answered his question, "there's people out there and they're calling my name." He walked over to the window and looked out. "There's nobody out there," he looked at me reassuringly and calmly spoke, "Why don't you just lay down and get some sleep." That was one swell idea. Get some sleep. Blot out the masses yelling up to me . . . yes, sleep is what the doctor ordered. But how? This part I could not figure but I said goodnight to Glen and gave it another try.

At first, I was scared, but then I thought the people outside were only admirers, disciples if you will, whose sole purpose was to see me set free. They were on my team trying to help. My only hope was that they didn't try a violent break-in to release me. But then I thought that there was no way anybody could break down those doors if I couldn't. With this secure thought, after a long time, I faded into a deep sleep. It was the first night I had slept on my own in about six days. No shot of Thorazine was necessary. This was a very good sign, but I was not out of the woods yet—I was entertaining some very wild hallucinations.

Chapter Nine

They let me sleep in the next day. Nobody woke me for breakfast and I barely made it to lunch. It was okay by me that I missed breakfast, I needed the sleep. It may have been the case that someone did try to wake me but I was too exhausted to move or even acknowledge the call. You can't even imagine how relieved I was to have slept on my own. I was starting to think I'd never be able to do that again.

The only thing on my busy schedule was to meet my psychiatrist late in the afternoon. I did, indeed, meet him after a few hours of shooting pool by myself, and later with pscyhe tech, Cliff. It was a lot of fun shooting pool with Cliff and it turns out he was an accomplished, first class man. He didn't even seem to mind me calling him Jimi Hendrix all the time. I did think he was Hendrix at first, but even after I knew better I continued to call him this as sort of an inside, running gag.

Cliff told me he went to Notre Dame on a four year football scholarship. He had been a tailback for Servite High School. When he got to Notre Dame, he didn't do as well at football, so he transferred to Cal. State Fullerton where he earned his degree in engineering. He also had his degree in something else (I can't remember what) but apparently his calling was working with troubled punks like us. I thought he was crazier than us to choose working with rowdies at lower pay than engineering. His stories about his degrees could have been fabricated but I seriously doubt it because he was too nice a guy to tell lies to someone fresh out of restraints. Either way, he was great to talk to and we opened up to each other while shooting stick.

"Do you know why you're here?" he asked me.

"No," this was my honest answer.

"Well . . . I have a pretty good idea," he spoke as he shot.

"What?" I was curious.

"Well, it seems to me that your life is pretty out of control right now."

I didn't understand, "What do you mean?"

"I mean your life is not in order right now. You're going through a crisis and it's going to take some time with the doctors before you can resume living your life normally." It was nice of him to tell me this because with my set of delusions, life seemed to be thriving. He was right of course, but me being the good little manic I was—I wasn't about to give up my delusions of grandeur. No way.

"Do you think I'll be here very long?" I asked reverently as I pocketed the eleven ball.

"That's up to the doctors," he paused, "but while you're here, take time to get yourself back together. You seem like a bright kid that's got a lot going for him." Again, he was right and I being the bright attentive kid that I was, took note of what the man was saying. I would have been able to have easily breezed through the whole process, but after he said this, I took stock of myself. I wasn't quite through with having fun with my delusions, but taking a deep look at who I was, and where I was going, would later become a very large and critical component of my stay.

The doctor I was to meet was John Stewart. We met for a half hour and in that time he described the whole process that would be implemented during my hospitalization. From meds to psychotherapy to school to occupational therapy. He also probed me about my life. I remember answering everything honestly but I'm hazy as to what was asked of me.

We met everyday for about a week and a half until he came to the conclusion that I was suffering from a disorder known as Bi-polar Affective Disorder (isn't it funny how the acronym of this term is B.A.D . . . Bi-polar Affective Disorder—THAT'S A BAD DISEASE . . . I get such a kick out of that, I sometime pee myself laughing . . . and I thought it up all by my lonesome) or Manic Depressive the older term. I prefer to be an MD, than someone suffering from B.A.D. Being called M.D. makes it sound as if I'm qualified to remove your spleen or something. Cool.

All in all, I liked the doctor but he was from Dallas and a hard core Cowboys fan, and I was from Philadelphia and a hard core Eagles fan. In this respect, we were natural enemies and at the time, we were both very serious about our football. Other than this one flaw, major as it was, I thought he was a nice, capable doctor. I felt I was in good hands.

That night between seven and nine, as on every night, the ward was open to visitors. Kim brought me two suitcases full of clothes. It was a welcomed relief, for I hadn't changed clothes since the Eisenhower administration and the fermentation process was well under way. Kim came alone and it gave us a chance to talk for awhile but it was painfully obvious that being in that place made her nervous. By now, I felt comfortable and I tried to make her feel more at home by introducing her around to the other kids. Linn Sue was glad to meet Kim because I told her all about old sis. Nonetheless, Kim still seemed nervous and wanted out of there.

I guess it's really difficult for a loved one to come into the environment of the hospital. It must also be a real task to come to acceptance about having a "nut" as a relative or friend. I wouldn't know, I'm the lucky bastard who gets to play the role of the nut. One good thing though, it gives me license to drool in public. As for Kim, I felt bad that she was in that position on my account. Let's face it, there is and probably always will be a strong social stigma associated with being mentally ill. It not only affects the mentally ill but the family and friends as well. My sister Kim as well as the rest of my family were in a precarious spot. I fully understood my sister's trepidation. It was a place I'm sure she never thought she'd be visiting. It was a place I was sure I'd never be visiting. Anyway, I guess the basic gist here is that the only thing a family can do is be as reassuring as possible. I'm glad I have a sister like Kim to bring me clothes and just talk. I would certainly do the same for her but I have faith that I won't have to. God, I'm hoping I never have to repay the debt I owe her.

After Kim left, Michael, a psyche tech, sat us down for assertion training. We did some role plays and during the second one, I got up, walked through the role play, went into my room, grabbed my bags and headed toward the big metal doors down the long corridor. Michael, who noticed this, continued on with his assertion training. I was ready to rock and roll as I stood by the big doors waiting for him to let me out of the dump. I had to be with Donna and it was time to go. After all, I was just a visitor . . . I had made a deal with Peter—one night. He gave me his word that it would be just one night and that long miserable night was long gone. It was time to go. I had to be with my beloved Donna. Did you hear me? I said, I had to be with my beloved Donna.

Michael let me stand there for quite awhile, until I started banging on the doors with both fists. At first he ignored the racket. I then banged harder and even kicked the door. I heard the kids laughing riotously but still no Michael. Then I began to verbalize—more like scream. "It's time to go!!!" The kids were wetting their diapers but still no Michael!! "I'm out of here!!!" I kicked and banged that door in a frenzy.

Finally, Michael came storming down the corridor and got right up in my face.

"What do you think you're doing?"

"Let me out of this fucking place!" I shouted in the man's face.

"You cannot leave," he spoke assertively.

"Look, I only agreed to stay here one night. It's been more than that. It's time to go!" I was firm.

"You cannot leave," he reiterated.

"Why not?" I asked belligerently. "I've got my bags and I'm ready to go."

"How are you going to get out?" he asked calmly.

"If you don't let me out, I'm going through that window," I pointed at the wired window in the door.

"Go ahead. I'd like to see that superman. Go ahead, why don't you put your head through it. I don't care if you get out or stay, but rest assured, I'm not letting you out." We were staring each other down.

"Go ahead, I'd like to see that," he continued to stare at me for awhile and then finally turned his back on me and walked back to the very interested kids.

I yelled, "I'm only a visitor here!"

He turned around and shot back, "yea, right!"

He gathered the wildly amused kids and resumed his role play.

I stood there for a moment, thinking. All the signs said get out of Dodge. I had one problem—I had no keys. BANG! I kicked the door. BANG! I kicked the door again. BANG! Again. Then, I started shaking that big metal mother. With each bang and shake I got more and more furious. The racket was unbelievable and now nobody was laughing. They knew I was in serious trouble. But I didn't give a shit, I wanted to get through that door and into the arms of Donna (the girl I hardly knew). I continued expending every ounce of fire on that monster while Michael, the bearded great, called up a few of my old buddies—The Goon Squad.

Yes, it was another fight with three or four massive dudes. Again, after a monumental struggle, I was finally overwhelmed and dragged into the restraint room where I was tied up like an animal. The whole time I kept screaming, "Donna!! Donna!! Donna!!" Marlon Brando had Stella—I had Donna.

It wasn't fair. Nothing was fair. And there I was—pissed off and in restraints again.

It is impossible to describe how insanely mad I was. I've never really been known for having a bad temper, but the times I was put in restraints, I was madder than anyone I've ever seen. This phenomenal anger was, of course, due to the manic depression and I had absolutely, positively, no control over myself. It's like I mentioned earlier, manics can be extremely funny, jovial and gregarious, but if you cross them in any way, they can become irritable and sometimes violent. In these restraint cases, I lost it entirely. That's rare, but it does happen now and again. Manics do have rages and they can become dangerous. The truly sad part is, the manic might be the kindest most gentle person in the world. But if the big red button is pushed he or she will burst.—Sad, very, very sad. Some of the nicest people in the world can become insanely violent and their reputations destroyed.

I lie in bed a defeated young man with nothing to show for

my expended energy but sore wrists and ankles. There is nothing more humiliating than being tied up against your will. I thrashed and thrashed as my mind reeled violently in a thousand different directions. As in the case of my other trips down restraint row, I fought until my strength was gone. I faded against my will, fearing death.

Once again, the next day was spent in seclusion. My delusions were still very much with me and an overwhelming sense of joy filled my insides as I sat thinking of how great my party was to be. After all I had been through, I had no reason to be that happy. I wasn't responding to the circumstances, I was responding to the disorder. The worst thing in the world could happen to me and ten minutes later I could be as happy as a clam entertaining odd, jovial delusions. Wheeee!

While I was in seclusion, I added to my list of cousins. First, and foremost, there was the great quarterback from the New Orleans Saints—Archie Manning. When I was a little boy, my father used to call him my cousin because we shared the same name—Archie. Find the logic there. Other famous figures, mostly sports heroes, were added as cousins and destined to be at the party. To name a few: there was Bobby Clarke of the Philadelphia Flyers; Rick Macleish of the Flyers; Bob Cousy of the Boston Celtics; Hank Aaron of the Atlanta Braves. As you can tell the same set of delusions was affecting me. If I liked someone who was a sports figure or rock and roll star, they were blood relatives. If you think about it, these delusions are understandable. After all, the life of a sixteen year old boy is full of rock and roll stars and sports heroes.

I entertained delusions about these people as I sat alone, bored mindless. If anything, I think this seclusion made my delusional network worse. I had too much time on my hands. On the flip side, the seclusion gave me time to calm down. From the authorities vantage, seclusion was the only answer to my problem. Banish the malcontents. In my case, I was a violent malcontent. And the only way out was to do everything by the book and become a perfect model citizen with a tattoo of the flag on my chest and crumbs from a piece of apple pie on the corners of my mouth. In other words be the good all American boy and calm my butt down. However, this was no easy task while you're juiced up on a manic high. How can you not be pumped out of your gourd when the greatest party of all time is being prepared especially for you? I was obsessed with the oddest part about the whole ordeal was that this was a natural state of mind for me. This was not drug induced. And this is why it was impossible for me to stop my behavior and thoughts. Nobody, including myself knew when I was going to stop behaving and thinking erratically.

I wasn't convinced that being a good boy was the best way

to go. I was higher than a kite and enjoying all of it except for being tied up. Think about how great it would be to have a high like this. To be all powerful—all knowing. To be able to do as you please and to be surrounded by all the true greats on the planet. Sanity be damned. This was great. Why give it up for reality? But at the time, reality was what was in my head. Paradoxical, yes, and in retrospect I wish I had never been sick in the first place. But every once in a while, I'll be walking down the street and a big smile will cross my face—how many people in this world have ever been that high naturally and felt the unbridled ecstasy and raw passion that I felt? Who cares about whether I was sane. It's an experience I'll never be able to forget. It's also an experience that cannot be explained with mere words. I've been attacking the subject for some time now and the only answer is that it must be experienced.

Of course, the price you pay for this high is enormous and life long lasting. Cocaine and heroin and all the other drugs are cheap compared to the price you pay for a good manic high. First off, you lose your sanity. How much is that worth to you darling?
Second—the doctors will tell you you've got it for life. You're on the rollercoaster from hell.
Third—Good news! Medicine can prevent the manic. Or then again it may not. Depends on whose lucky. Spin that wheel. Roll that dice.
Fourth—Even when the medicine is working, the side effects are, as they say down at the shipyard, a pain in the ass. Causes drowsiness, diarrhea, dizziness, confusion and about forty other things I'm too drowsy to remember.
Fifth—You have to buy the stuff. Normal people don't have to buy their sanity. And let's not forget the doctors and psychologists.

You get the idea.

One hell of a price is paid to keep sanity. But believe me it's a price worth paying even if you do fall out of the boat once in a while.

They let me out of seclusion the next morning after all the other kids went off to school. I shot pool with Cliff most of the morning and the first thing he said to me was, "I heard about last night."

"Yea," I said quietly.

"You know," he paused as he shot, "there is only one way out of here."

"How?" I asked unknowingly.

"You have to play by the rules," he said.

"But I've got to get to Donna," I stammered.

"Who's Donna?" he asked.

"My wife to be," I said proudly.

"Your what?!" he was awfully surprised. "Aren't you a little young to be getting married?" I didn't answer. "How long have you been going out with this girl?"

"Well we've never actually gone out."

"What?!" he was shocked, "you've never gone out with this girl and you're convinced you're going to marry her?" I shrugged and he replied, "You mean to tell me that all of this is over a crush on a girl you've never dated?" Boom! Reality! He had hit the nail on the head. A good portion of my problems revolved around the delusions I held for a girl I barely knew and had a schoolboy crush on.

Cliff continued, "Maybe you should stop thinking about this girl and get your head together. At your age you should be looking at a lot of different girls."

"But I'm madly in love with her," I spoke the truth.

"Surely there must be other girls you're interested in," he paused. "How about the girls on the ward, there must be one you like," he paused again, "I don't mean become obsessed with them—that's unhealthy. I mean flirt, interact. That's about the speed of people your age."

"Linn Sue," I said shyly.

"What?" he asked.

"Linn Sue," I paused. "I think she's cute."

"Now there you go! You do have another interest. You're not as obsessed as I was led on to believe," he took a shot and missed. "My man has good taste . . . I've been eyeing that Linn Sue myself. She's quite a cutie and nice, too."

"Yea," I smiled, "but I don't know how to act around cute girls."

"Just be yourself," he laughed.

Just be yourself. I've heard that one before. When you're sixteen years old it's hard enough to know who you are because your identity as an adult is just starting to be formed. Compound this with your new found friend, manic psychosis, and the question of who you are looms paramount. What is your opening line to a girl, "Hey baby, I'm nuts . . . what do you say you and me hit a movie. I hear 'Psycho' is playing at the Bellview." It doesn't work. But then something critical dawned on me. Linn Sue and I were in the same boat and she really seemed to respond to me. There was truly no reason for me to pretend or act for this girl like I had to for the rest. Hell, the girl saw me carted off, tied up and locked into an isolation chamber. Maybe my good buddy Cliff was right. Maybe I shouldn't put all my eggs in one basket. But then again, switching love interests was no easy task for a guy wrought with delusions and obsessed. I'm either cursed or blessed by loyalty, I'm not sure which.

The kids started returning one by one and sure enough, Linn Sue was up for a game of pool. Cliff excused himself with a knowing smile as Linn Sue took over his spot. I'm sure he got a big kick out of Linn Sue coming right up to me.

We played pool, laughed and flirted like mad with one another. When I was with this girl, the memory of Donna would start to fade, but ultimately it would return in droves. I was and am an extremely stubborn little devil and I was not to give up my crush on Donna. Still, Linn Sue was seen in a different light following my talk with Cliff. I mean, I wasn't cheating on Donna. I was free to flirt with Linn Sue. And, indeed, I continued to flirt with Linn Sue in my own shy way. My off the wall sense of humor and boyish charm kept on warming that beautiful heart of Linn Sue. My heart was getting a bit warm itself.

Chapter Ten

My parents came to visit me that night and I lied. I told them everything was okay. Indeed, everything was not okay. The night before, I slept in leather straps. Yet, when someone asks you how everything is going, you usually say fine and move on to some form of small talk. The small talk in this case was about how fine I was. The conversation did pick up, however, when my stepfather asked me if I knew why I was where I was.

"No," I replied. "I don't even know where I am." I knew.

"Son," he said softly and slightly shaking, "you're in the hospital. You're very sick."

"What's so sick about me? I feel great." This was a half truth.

"Son," he continued firmly, "you're not thinking clearly. You need time to work things out."

"What's to work out, Pa? All I want to do is go home. I haven't done anything wrong," I pleaded a little.

"No," he agreed, "you haven't done anything wrong, but you're not thinking straight. You're making up all these stories that aren't true and you're scaring the hell out of all of your friends. They're worried sick about you. They've called us and we've called around, and everyone agrees that you're acting strangely. Now, it's our duty to keep you here until you're thinking straight again." He paused and grabbed my mother's hand. I knew the man meant business—his hands were shaking which was always the tell tale sign. "We both love you very much and we want to see you get better soon so that you can come home."

BLASPHEME. How dare he say my stories were made up. Maybe he wasn't invited to my party for some reason. Maybe he was a traitor of some sort and had taken my mother hostage.

This, of course, was totally absurd. I was around the bend on that idea. My stepfather is a great guy and on my side at all times. But my delusions were so strong I couldn't see reality. These delusions owned me, and now they stood between me and my stepfather. As far as I was concerned, these delusions stood and he was talking blasphemous gibberish.

It's this form of stubbornness that is the cornerstone of a manic high. When you're in this state you simply do not want to let go of your delusions of grandeur. You hold on to them even if it means alienating a strong relationship. You accept what your head tells you because your head is telling you the most delicious lies, and you feel better than you ever have. I believed all the lies and would have done anything my head told me. If it told me to jump off a building, I would have jumped off a building. Fortunately for me, there were no evil thoughts, for I might have acted on them. All of my delusions were about how I was the greatest guy on earth.

That night, after interacting with the other kids for awhile, I entertained my delusions in my own room before lights out. I had been given medication to help me sleep and to help alleviate my delusions, but it didn't seem to be working. I lie on my bed obsessing about my party . . . the same old song and dance. I was as convinced as ever that the party would take place soon and I would be initiated into an elite group of people that I considered great.

Lights out finally came and I did, indeed, try to sleep. However, that damned generator across the compound was blasting and made sleep impossible. I lie there in bed, trying desperately to sleep and low and behold, the auditory and visual hallucinations re-emerged. I heard a loud clanging outside as if somebody were emptying the trash. I got up out of bed and looked across the compound. It was Archie Manning!!! I couldn't believe it! I started screaming at the top of my lungs, "Archie!!! Archie!!! Whooo hoo!!! Alright Arch!!!" When Archie heard me he ducked down out of sight. He didn't want to blow his cover, because it was his job to spring me from the steely claws of the hospital. He was there to save me as if I were his little brother. He was gonna be the dude to take me to the party. I was sure of this.

The noise I was making was enough to bring in Glen who seemed a touch wary of me. "What's all the noise in here?"

I didn't want to blow Archie's cover so I said, "I thought I saw someone I knew out there."

He looked out the window and saw no one. "There's nobody out there. Now just lay down and try to get some sleep. The medicine should be kicking in soon," he left.

I tried to sleep again, but again I heard the trash cans clinking. I looked out the window and saw Archie again and this time he winked at me as if he were trying to signal me or something. I began screaming, "What's that Arch?!!!" I didn't understand. "What's that mean?!!!" Archie then ducked down, disappearing on the runway by the generator.

Big Glen came back in, this time with an irritated smirk and more medicine for the great Archie boy, king of the night. I took the medicine and promised to be quiet. Indeed, I remained quiet. I sat on the little desk by the window waiting for Archie to return. He never returned and I grew sullen waiting for him. There was a little pencil in the desk and I started writing all over the desk in huge letters—WHY? Why? Why was I put in this place? Why? Why did I have to be the one to carry the weight of the world? Why? Why wasn't I allowed to do all the things I wanted to do? Why? Why wasn't I allowed out of this place? Why? Why was I the one to be disturbed and distracted? Why not someone else?

There were a million whys and no answers. I sat around on the desk and began to fade with the distant sound of people sneaking around the compound. They were my disciples waiting for my release. I grew so tired, wary and dejected that I flopped myself on the bed and cried myself to sleep, knowing full well that I'd been spending another day in a mental hospital.

The next day, the doctors of the staff set up a schedule for me to follow for the remainder of my stay in the hospital. I was to go to therapy three times a week, and occupational therapy for an hour everyday. Also, I was to go to school everyday in the room that we ate in. There were two certified teachers who aided me through all of the subjects I was supposed to be enrolled in at my high school. At the end of each week they'd give out honors for the student of the week. I won almost every week and my courses were more elaborate than the other kids. This didn't mean a whole lot because the other kids didn't care about school.

A typical day? First, we woke up and showered if we wanted (some showered at night), and went to breakfast. Then we attended rounds which is where all the doctors, staff and patients got together and discussed the day to come and anything that was an issue. After rounds, we'd play volleyball in the courtyard. After this, our schedules varied. Some went to therapy in the morning, others went to school. Then, in the afternoon we'd switch. I had morning therapy and afternoon school. Fortunately for both Linn Sue and I, we had opposite schedules. I've never been able to study next to a girl or woman I'm attracted to. That's probably why I did well in the all boys Catholic school in Pennsylvania. None of the other boys smelled like that perfume Charlie. Anyway, our days were always full.

On this particular day, my first on the schedule, the thing I remember most vividly was our volleyball game. This was the first chance I had to be with all the kids and staff at once, and I really wanted to show off my athletic ability, particularly for an A-1 Chinese young lady. In this manic state, my athletic ability was at its peak, and I remember doing very well. I was jumping higher than I've ever jumped with the possible exception of the night I almost dunked that basketball (that one hurts to this day). I spiked everything when I was at the net and I dove on asphalt to save everything else. I vividly remember facing old Cliff at the net. We were natural rivals, him being a big stud of an athlete and me being the pixy Peter Pan who suffered always from the Davey and Goliath syndrome. We'd both go up for the ball at the same time and hit the ball at the same time. Then we'd both come down laughing. Sometimes he'd score, other times I'd score but it really didn't matter because we'd both be too busy laughing and ribbing each other. After each time Willie scored, Linn Sue would pick up the ball, walk over to me, hand me the ball, smile and walk away without saying a word. I was starting to fall in love.

The volleyball games, as I recall, were the most relaxed, communal part of the day. We were a bunch of kids, both young and old, celebrating the joy of competition and good clean fun. Everyday I looked forward to volleyball and shooting pool. They were integral in my journey back to sanity and once I was sane again, these two activities helped keep me there. Distractions in the hospital were essential. Even the television kept you from brooding about the seriousness of your situation.

Another distraction, as I mentioned earlier, was the friendships you made with one another. You were in the same boat, and often times it felt as if that boat were sinking. The only thing you could do is hang on to one another, otherwise you felt desperate and doomed.

Fortunately, I made friends quickly and fit right into the machinery of the sub culture. There was some, like Tony, that I never liked or got along with, but for the most part I got along famously with everyone. This is probably why I only spent three months as compared to the four that was predicted by the authorities.

If you made enemies on the ward, as did Tony, or alienated yourself, as did Rich, your stay in the hospital was a lonely, painful one and most probably a longer one. Both Tony and Rich were in the hospital when I arrived and still there when I left. I honestly believe that the doctors watched how well you interacted with the others in your surroundings. That seemed to be how they determined how well you were doing. So, getting out was contingent on how well you adjusted. You had to give the doctors what they wanted if you were to be released.

NOTE: On making friends—although we were all problem children, it was immediately evident to me, once I came around, that we were all very "normal kids" in most ways. We each desired the same things that any "normal" kid does. We wanted love and understanding. That's why we became friends so quickly. If nobody could give us these things, we could give them to each other.

When I first met my psychoanalyst, I was very nervous and more than skeptical about the whole process. I refused to believe that any old shrink could help me at all. After all, there was nothing wrong with me. In fact, I had everything going for me. I was about to be indoctrinated into an elite group of great people. And I was to be the greatest of them all. Why would I need therapy? The only reason I agreed to see her was because I didn't want to wind up on a bed wearing leather straps.

So, I met with Dr. Margaret Eberhauser. She was a very somber, stoic looking lady about forty-two years old. I knew from the start that working with this woman would be futile. She was way too serious for me. I needed more upbeat and outgoing. In the manic state, the last thing the manic wants is someone somber and stoic. But Margaret was who was assigned to me and I tried to stick it out.

On that first time we met, she almost immediately asked me the same question everyone was asking of me, "Do you know why you're here Archie?"

Of course I did, "Yes, you're holding me until it's time to go to my party."

"What party?" she asked concerned.

"Oh, come on, you know as well as everyone else. My coming out party."

"Your coming out party?" This chick was stone faced as if Rodin created her himself.

"Yes," I said belligerently, "my coming out party."

"Why don't you tell me about this party?"

I sat with my arms folded across my chest. I refused to answer such an asinine question. She knew as well as the rest.

"Archie?" she tried to engage me. "Archie, you don't have to say anything if you don't want. I just thought I could help you sort things out."

"Well you can't!" I snapped. "Why do you people keep jerking me around!!?" Oh, I was right up in her face with that one and she was taken aback by the fury of my reply. I can get this really nasty look on my face when I'm mad and I'm sure old stoneface was close to losing her bladder. I don't think she was prepared for the likes of me.

There was a long period of silence before she asked me the next question. I'm sure she wanted to end the session after my outburst, but it was her duty to carry on with the session.

"Archie, do you have any idea where you are?"

"No," I said sarcastically, "where am I?"

She looked at me with her stony orbs and said, "You're in the hospital."

"I know that, but why? What have I ever done to deserve this? I've always been good."

"It's not a matter of whether you deserve it or not, Archie."

"Well, then what's it a matter of?" This was a legitimate question.

She looked me right in the eye and said, "You are not thinking and functioning normally and we want to help you get back on track before we let you go."

That statement almost literally sent me through the roof. I frantically jumped up and started kicking the door, "Why does everybody keep saying shit like that?" I started crying, "I'm a good person. No! I'm a great person! I could be one of the greatest of all time if you assholes wouldn't keep holding me back. Just let me go! Let me be free!" I was pleading to her, but I knew she wouldn't let me go, particularly after I yelled at her and kicked the door like a madman. I stopped pleading and sat down calmly. Why I didn't just take off and make a run for it, I don't know. Or maybe I do know—down deep I knew there was something wrong.

However, the old delusional network still had a grip on me and my reality was far nicer than reality. I wanted to bolt more than anything in the world, but I was too confused to do anything. What the hell was I to do?

There was a long, drawn out, dead silence in that depressing room. Margaret was letting me calm down. I'm sure she didn't want to provoke me in fear of my lashing out against her. I never have and never will hit a woman, but how would she know that at the time.

"Are you okay now?" she spoke softly.

"Yes." I felt guilty. "I'm sorry about snapping out. I'm not normally like this."

"That's okay, we all lose it once in awhile." Old Stony actually had a pretty nice smile, "I think we've done enough for the first time. Maybe on Thursday you'll feel comfortable enough to talk a little more. I'm here to listen—you can tell me anything about anything. As for now, why don't you go back to the ward and think of the things you want to talk about on Thursday." With that, I said my goodbyes and went back to the ward as confused as I'd ever been.

So that was therapy; throw a few tirades, scare the shit out of the therapist and come back on Thursday.

I did get one thing out of that brief session. I began to question, ever so gently, my delusions of grandeur. Maybe they weren't real after all. Maybe there was no party. Maybe I'm not so great. Maybe I'm just another ordinary Schmo. Maybe I'm just another ordinary, psychotic Schmo. Maybe the therapy session did some good. Maybe. However, the delusions continued to roll on—destination unknown.

Chapter Eleven

When I went back to the ward, I played pool with Linn Sue and Julie. I was still a little worked up by the therapy session but it's easy to calm down when you're playing pool with two beautiful girls. If we were in high school, I don't think I'd have the courage to approach such beautiful girls. I'm naturally shy around them, but when you're locked up with them it's not easy to run and hide. It was refreshing to interact with them and as I said earlier, something was definitely abrew with myself and Linn Sue.

It's interesting to point out that most every girl I saw come through the hospital was physically beautiful. I suppose beautiful girls have it tougher than average looking girls. Maybe it's because at the age of sixteen every jerk with hormones is sitting high above them like a vulture ready to swoop down and take them away. I don't know, all I do know is that I felt like Hugh Hefner when I strolled though all those rubber rooms late at night, in my swinging beige bathrobe. I wish I had a pipe.

Anyway, as I was playing with these girls, a delusion raced to me. It was a very odd delusion revolving around the number eleven. It was a delusion that lasted an awfully long time, and to this day I'm not sure it was a delusion—and if it was I wasn't sure at the time what it meant. It began when I remembered an old girlfriend's birthday. She was born 11-11-66 and I was officially put into the hospital on 11-11-80. But that really wasn't what started the eleven delusion. The eleven delusion started whenever I looked at a clock. I always looked up at 11 minutes past or at 11:11, etc . . . The last pool ball was always the eleven if it wasn't knocked in first. I don't exactly know what this meant but I became fixated with the number eleven and this fixation lasted for as long as I was on that first manic high. Mind you, I'm not a superstitious man by nature but this delusion stuck and it literally started driving me crazy. The truth remained though, when I looked up at the clock there was some kind of eleven involved. To this day, when I see eleven past or 11:11, I think this delusion is following me. Very strange.

NOTE: This is the strangest note I'll write concerning this text. The number eleven showed up later in research when researcher Janice A. Egeland et. al, through researching the homogeneous Ahmish communities of Lancaster, PA., cited that the disorder might be found on the eleventh chromosome. My old college buddy, Danny Clancy, who is getting his Ph.D. in the sciences, used to keep up with the hunt for what causes Manic Depression. He knew all about my fixation on the number eleven and we both got a good laugh out of the latest research. But then I started to question . . . and question some more. Was it possible that I knew innately the exact origin of my disorder? I used to be the type to immediately dismiss such nonsense, but after having several "breakdowns" and all the hallucinations, you become a little more open minded. Maybe I knew the disorder was on the eleventh chromosome and maybe the discredited research has solid merit. Another point, I pretty much knew I was dying when I was ten and ruptured my spleen. Is it possible for the human mind to know, subconsciously, what is going on with the body at all times? Does the computer know itself? Can it diagnose and cure itself? Questions.

This was the delusion I entertained whilst I whipped the hineys off of my beautiful new house mates. Although the delusion persisted while I was playing pool, this did not stop me from flirting like mad. It was amazing to me that I could flirt and laugh and joke with these girls when normally I was very shy with them. And the great part is that they thought everything I said was funny. And the even greater part is that, indeed, everything I did say was funny. In this, the manic state, my sense of humor was wildly funny and off the wall. This good humor was infectious and it seemed as if most everyone wanted to be around me. I call this the "walking party" facet of a good, solid manic high. You walk into a room and you're so animated and hilarious that a party breaks out all around you. Everyone is invited. This is probably the greatest feature of the high, but very few people can sustain it forever. However, I see many good comedians who I'm sure are at least slightly manic and can sustain this buzz long enough to make a living out of being funny and inventive. Again, however, with most full blown manics this "walking party" is broken up by devastating depression after the manic goes over the top.

That evening while lying around on the living room floor, the delusion of the party came back to me. I had been talking with Dave and Craig and I began thinking out loud. "Hey, wait a minute, that makes Jim Morrison my cousin. Great! that means he'll be at the party too." That was pretty off the wall and Craig started laughing hysterically for some odd reason. He said laughingly, "You know, you really are nuts!" The dumb grunt knew how to state the obvious. Jim Morrison had been dead for ten years, but no matter, he'd be at the party. And Hendrix would be standing right next to him. The two of them had been hiding out for the past ten years or so waiting for me to come of age. Yes, that is correct. Then they would resurface at the same time—wouldn't that be wonderful? I was out in left field . . . no, no, I take that back, I was in foul territory.

It's truly sad that these grand delusions were never to materialize . . . they were only the beautiful visions of a sick, seriously disturbed youth. I postulate a question now: Is it truly sick to want beautiful things to happen? In this case it didn't make a difference what the answer was to that question. The fingers had already been pointed at me and I was already labeled "seriously disturbed."

And as I have said earlier, these delusions were my reality. So, for the time being, in the head of disturbed youth, reality was painted with an array of different colors that no one else could perceive. Indeed, as Craig had so astutely pointed out, I was nuts. At least that's what everyone was saying. But then again, what if my reality was the one true reality and everyone else in their almighty sobriety was wrong? Argue that one for awhile. I did. I'm stubborn. I argued that point for a couple more weeks by continuing to entertain these delusions. Stubbornness, I would have to say, is one of the cornerstones of a juicy, manic high. Giving up the delusions and giving up the high is seen as absurdity to the manic. Why throw out the greatest feelings you've ever felt? No, by all means, slap on some more hefty dreams. Even if you wind up in the hospital, keep the delusions coming. What can they do—feed you and give you a place to sleep? My folks were fully covered. This is how the manic thinks and acts—don't let go of whatever it was that was stimulating the limbic system in a positive vein.

The first manic high is the greatest. The reason being, with the subsequent highs you remember the ramifications of the first high. There are plenty of ramifications. The most obvious of these is, of course, incarceration. If you let your disorder get out of control you will most probably wind up in either a hospital, halfway house or jail. Roll the dice . . . take a pick . . . It ain't pretty but it sure is the truth. Even the most highly respected and educated people on the face of the earth can wind up in one of these places. Oh, I also forgot death—either by suicide or murder. The latter is not a joke. In some manic confrontations, violence breaks out and the manic might attack even if the other person is armed (often times a police officer) and the manic can be killed. I've read more than one such report and had a confrontation or two with the police in subsequent highs. It's an inability to stop, and to be fair to the manic, it's beyond control.

I mean, the hospital is the place to be and all—particularly with all those beautiful lasses and hip swinging multi-colored rubber chairs. However, in earnest, it's definitely not the place to be. There are crazy people in the hospital . . . (I was hoping Judy Garland would pop out of one of those rubber chairs, introduce me to Toto and take me to the land of fucking OZ). Do you want to be one of these crazy people? No . . . Nay . . . Nada! On the first high, you are not aware of the fact that you are being incarcerated for not being exactly "sane," as it were. So, this is why the first one is the best. On later highs, you understand what a pain in the ass the hospital really is and you immediately do anything to get the hell out of there—even if that means behaving. Of course, after you are hospitalized for the first time, you're stuck with the stigma of being mentally ill. The knowledge that you are chemically "different" than others is sunk in every day of your life when you take that medicine that makes you drowsy and pee more than anybody alive or dead. So, Manics want as little to remind them that they are permanently ill as possible. Ergo, they want nothing to do with manic highs. The aftermath is too much to deal with and everyday you're not in the hospital or jail is a silent triumph.

Okay. After talking with the guys for awhile I looked at the clock, and it read 8:11. That, of course, was very significant and in this particular instance it meant it was time for a bath. The eleven thing always signified something but it could be a little stupid, something like get up and take a pee. It was nonetheless significant.

I went to my room to put on my pajamas and bathrobe. I then went to the unoccupied boys bathroom. This is when I was hit with a wave full of delusions and hallucinations. I heard a huge crowd of people applauding me from outside. Yes! They were my disciples roaring in approval of my decision to take a bath. I envisioned a hidden camera somewhere in the bathroom and a huge screen taking up the whole side of the building. The huge throng of my disciples saw every move I made in that bathroom. I decided to do a little dance for them as I laughed hysterically . . . the old strip tease play on two. First, off came the bathrobe. The crowd roared and whooped like I had never heard before. Second, I stripped off the top of my pajamas very slowly and sensually like a stripper would. The song "the stripper" began blaring through the compound as the masses screamed, whistled and laughed their approval. Then came the pants and underwear as quickly as possible and then bang, into the tub as quick as possible before the throngs could get a glimpse of my treasured genitalia or a gander at my secondary sex characteristics. Mama raised me right. The crowd could only see from the top of the tub.

I laughed in hysterics as I taunted the crowd by sticking my tongue out at the wall next to the tub where the hidden camera was located. Half the crowd applauded my discretion and were proud that I knew what was happening. The other half of the crowd booed my ass off. They wanted to see their hero in the raw. PERVERTS!

I played in the tub, splashing the water around . . . then, I began singing Neil Young tunes to the crowd at the top of my lungs. . . . The crowd outdoors was going nuts while I belted out old Sugar Mountain in its entirety and the fans went bonkers, baby! They were all having the time of their lives as I entertained them in the sudsy raw. This was one helluva party, boy!!! My fans were just dying to have me come out and join them. I wanted to oblige, knowing full well it was not time yet, but something told me those nuts knew the exact time I'd be released. And at that given time, they were all going to converge at the site of the party and I would have no trouble finding the festivities. Everyone I had ever known and remotely liked would be there waiting for my triumphant release from the hospital. I'm telling you right here, right now—this was one hell of a trip! The greatest feeling on earth! I was higher than any kite, and I didn't need any drugs to get there. Yes, yes, yes, it was all natural, all real, and all mine! Yes!

Singing in the bathtub not only entertained the crowd outside but the crowd within as well. When I finally came out of the bathroom (fully dressed, of course), I was greeted by Linn Sue and Julie. They were laughing. Linn Sue looked at me and asked, "Was that you singing Archie?"

I laughed and smiled proudly, "Yes, it was, what did you think?"

She laughed and smiled broadly, "I think it sucked, Archie."

We stood there a moment smiling broadly and staring into each others eyes. What a babe! The silent romance rolled along merrily and sweetly. I knew my woman to be was Ms. Donna Seznick, but you can't fault a guy for innocently flirting during times of warfare. The relationship between Linn Sue and me was akin to cold war. We both had our fingers on the big red button but neither of us pushed. But we were both jubilantly aware of how we felt about each other. Man, what a great feeling to have a beautiful girl attracted to you.

That night as I lay in bed, I was relaxed and smiling. I had never felt more at peace in my young life. I had figured everything out and was enjoying the feeling of knowing everything about my impending greatness. This is the part of the manic phase that is simply irreplaceable and irresistible. The inner peace was not to be believed and certainly unparalleled. This is the reason the manic doesn't want to let go of his high. When the circumstances are right, there is no such thing as a better sensation. The serenity, albeit based firmly on an untruth, is phenomenal.

I smiled myself to sleep. Glen hadn't the need to worry about me on this night. Life was a leisure cruise in the Bahamas.

Chapter Twelve

The next day was spent for the most part in isolation. I wasn't in trouble or anything, it just so happened to be Saturday and all the other kids were home on weekend passes. On this particular weekend all the other kids were gone. Apparently, the kids were all good during the week except for the king of infractions and erratic behavior—the great Archie McRae. I hadn't scored enough points or served enough time to be released . . . not even to the cognizance of my highly reliable and respected parents. The three trips to the isolation chamber was enough assurance that I wasn't going for a trip in my pa's beautiful brown Audi. I don't think they would have let me go even if I was good. After all it was my first week as a farmer.

Nonetheless, I was alone with the staff all weekend. All I did was shoot pool and think. I had ample time to think about where I was and why I was there. It didn't make sense to me. Why was I being punished for being a great guy? I knew where I was but I couldn't tell you why I was there. At this point in the game I still didn't know I was a manic depressive or even that I was sick. It's amazing that I didn't know what was happening to me. The fact that the delusions of grandeur and feelings of superiority were still with me and made it literally impossible for me to understand why I was incarcerated.

The answer was easy enough—I was very sick. However, I wasn't about to subscribe to this theory. I still firmly believed that everyone was out preparing a party of unequaled proportions for me. They were only holding me until the time when the party was ready. Then I'd be set free to do whatever it was whenever I wanted to do it. This theory made sense to me and was much more palatable than reality.

Of course on other occasions I completely ignored the fact that I was in a mental hospital. I would tell myself that I was in the Navy or at the University of Notre Dame and I would honestly and wholeheartedly believe these deceptions. The God awful truth was much easier to deal with when you made up stories about where you were and why you were there. This of course only contributed to the difficulty of making the long journey back to reality. My own reality made much more sense to me, was a lot more fun and kept the delusional network ball rolling. Isn't it nicer to believe that you are truly great rather than truly disturbed?

My denial ran rampant that first weekend of isolation. I shot pool the whole time and thought elatedly about how I was the best at everything. Anybody who had ever known would be shocked by this new found confidence because I always had a tendency to put myself down. The latter had always been my basic nature.

The delusion of the party continued to roll through my head as I played patiently and happily. I had ample time to add a few more "cousins" to the guest list. In essence, what I was doing was fortifying the walls that I had already built as obstacles to reality. Being alone was definitely not good for me because instead of calming me down, it geared me up. Sure, I was well behaved, but my head was reeling ideas all over my cranial cavity. And at this juncture there was nobody to chip away at the wall of delusions. Old Stone Face made a gallant start but I got out the old mortaring equipment and filled in the cracks in the wall when nobody was around. In other words, being alone without communication or action made my brand of insanity worse.

A long road to recovery lay in front of me; yet, again, I still believed in my delusions. However, there were also those moments of perfect clarity when I saw clearly where I was and why I was there. But then I'd run and hide behind those massive, well masoned walls. The eminent question for everyone, I suppose, was would I ever accept the social definition of reality again?

For quite a while I thought about what all this nonsense was doing to my family and friends. It must have been extremely difficult to watch a so called "normal" loved one have a complete and total nervous breakdown. The odd part about it was that a week earlier it could have been me watching someone else break. I sure in the hell would be extremely concerned about my friends or family members breaking. Then I thought about how my mother must be feeling—my God! Then I was confused again, then I ran and hid behind the wall of delusions. This was my pattern.

There was one pressing question that came to me while I shot pool . . . why me? The answer to this of course is why not me? That's what it all boils down to . . . who's the lucky bastard who wins the nervous breakdown lottery. Unfortunately, I'd never be the same again. My life was to be altered forever.

Chapter Thirteen

The next week was spent getting acclimated to the daily grind of the hospital. I was still busy entertaining delusions, but I was also beginning to realize where I was and why I was there. The main instrument in bringing me around was the therapy. Therapy made me start to think that there was something wrong with me. The first question that came to my mind during these first few sessions was, "Why am I talking to this stone faced lady about my life?" The answer was, of course, I was forced to be there. But then I asked myself, "Why am I being forced?" The only answer I could come up with was that it was general consensus that I be in therapy. Of course, they were right but at the time I was questioning how sane the sane were. I mean, who were they and how did they know whether what was going on in my head was sanity or insanity? Were these people God? Nonetheless, I sort of enjoyed therapy from the very beginning. It feels good to be able to talk about anything you want and know full well that what was being said was purely confidential.

In one of the first sessions, I began to talk about my beloved Donna Seznick only to realize that I had hardly even spoken to her and that my crush on her was a massive delusion I had built around her and it was as if she had a massive fortress built around her. From the very beginning of speaking about her it hit me in the face that this girl was just an adolescent infatuation. Or was it? I saw very clearly and then not so clearly. I held on to my delicious delusion for at least awhile longer . . . I mean, anything in this life can happen, right? Are you going to tell me otherwise? And who might you be?

Although I hung on to the delusion as long as I could, a shadow of doubt started to emerge. It took me a long time to come to grips with the first and one simple truth that Donna Seznick and I had no love founded for each other. Only one of us saw the other as being special, and the other, didn't know the other existed.

Doctor Eberhauser began to slowly and systematically pry my life apart piece by piece. I'm sure it must have been very difficult for her to shed light on the truth. I was very guarded about the truth in my life and the details of my delusional network. After all, I assumed that everyone knew of my greatness and my story in general. So why talk about it? I didn't like discussing my brilliance and wonderful future with average ordinary schmoes. Humility was another strength of mine. As far as the real truth is concerned, it wasn't clear to me this early in the ball game. One of the first barrages of questions asked was about my family. How was my relationship with my mother? . . . great. How was my relationship with my father? . . . great. Okay, can I go home now? No, Archie, you must continue to eat that wonderful hospital food for another two and a half months.

I honestly believed that the knowledge of my greatness was common knowledge shared commonly and innately by one and all. I also thought that I was the only person on the face of the earth who possessed all the secrets of the universe. I was not about to give up any of these secrets to old stoneface.
NOTE: DELUSIONS OF GRANDEUR! HELLO! PARANOIA! HELLO! NAIVETE, INNOCENCE, BLIND FAITH, STUBBORN-NESS! HELLO, HELLO, HELLO, HELLO!!!! Need I say more?

I was very much the challenge for Dr. Eberhauser. She had a very easy time of helping me with my love life or alleged love life but I wouldn't give her any details on anything personal. She did indeed help with sorting out my thoughts about Donna, and it was her idea that I confront Donna (which I did later) but for the most part I did not open up to this woman.

No ma'am. I didn't envy Doctor Eberhauser's position. I wouldn't have wanted me as a patient. For one thing, I was very emotional and prone to outbursts of a violent nature. If I got pissed off I'd get up and start beating the snot of her big green door. Oh yea, on more than one occasion I'd get up and just start kicking and punching the door. Believe me, I was a frightening little baboon when I let go and I let go several times with Dr. Eberhauser. It felt great!
NOTE: Again I'm not violent by nature except for when I was in this state. However, since I was in this state and a tad violent, Doctor Eberhauser asked me if I wanted a male doctor. She wasn't getting anything out of me and I'm quite sure that I scared her with my outbursts. Come to think of it I remember her eyes popping out of her head one time when I violently kicked her scale when she asked me a question about my father. She scrambled all around the floor looking for her eyeballs and when she finally found them and popped them back in her sockets, she ended the session for the day. I'm sure the mad scramble made her realize that she really wasn't helping the old Archman or herself. I felt kind of bad that it had to end . . . after all, she was nice. She also had nice tibia and fibula combinations on each leg which were usually covered with white nylons. Not bad gamms for an old stone face. I'll say no more.

I think what I most liked about therapy was that you could purge your soul and not have to worry about the ramifications of what was said. You could say anything you wanted without having to worry about what you said leaking out to other people. Also, the therapist gives you feedback and tries to add insight into solving your unique problems. There is an enormous freedom in this relationship as long as the therapist is suited to the patient and vice versa. Once you have the proper match, the relationship will grow founded on trust, and a freedom that doesn't exist anywhere else will develop. Not even your closest friends know as much about you as a good therapist. I found this to be enormously enticing and often times I felt completely liberated after a good session. However, in my earlier sessions with Eberhauser, I wasn't about to give away all my trade secrets. I only talked about things on a personal level. I wasn't going to bring my cousins into this picture. The decision not to discuss my cousins was a beautiful maneuver that kept my delusional network in tact. In fact, I kept the delusions a secret because I was afraid that I'd lose the network entirely. And that's what made my life so great—my delusions. Just my imagination alone was worth more than all the gold in the world. I wasn't about to let go, but as the days wore on, I was beginning to understand more fully that I was ill and needed help.

The interesting thing about the illness of manic depression is that you can feel better than you have in your entire life, and ever will, and still be considered as being severely ill. When I was forced into therapy, I thought there was nothing wrong. How can you be ill when you're on top of the world? This is a paradoxical dilemma the manic must face and come to grips with. The manic must admit there is something wrong with him. Gradually, or sooner the better, it must be done. This is probably the hardest thing for the manic to do—letting go of that precious high.

Meanwhile back on the ward that second week, it became evident to me that Tony, the boy that crossed me for no reason, was just a bad seed. He would pull stunts on people that were just downright nasty. For example, he urinated in the shampoo bottle of all the boys he didn't like. Fortunately, I was not one of those guys, but it was a mark for me to keep my distance. There was no reason to invite any kind of attention from him at all particularly since I had tied the restraint record with the beautiful Miss Linn Sue. I was still wavering emotionally and any kind of wrong move by Tony would surely send my fists rocketing toward his ugly face. Oddly, I knew this even in the state I was in, so I played it smart and stayed away from him. When he walked into a room I was in, I immediately left without so much as a word.

The rest of the guys, who the trick was played on, vowed to get back at that swine Tony. So, during that second week in the hospital I witnessed a pack of adolescents exchange nasty little trickery with one another. It was very immature and it made me very paranoid since I was the new kid on the block. They didn't come at me though. Maybe they thought I'd snap again. They were probably right. Anyway, the shenanigans didn't last too long . . . Donny, with the help of the beautiful Linn Sue, passed off a whole bar of ex-lax as being an exquisite chocolate from France. Donny bet Tony the chocolate against Tony's two Hershey bars that Linn Sue could beat him at pool. Linn Sue was pretty good and gave Donny a scare, but she hacked the last couple of shots and let Tony win. Tony was of course a sexist as well as being an all around asshole, and as such bragged to Linn Sue about how much better men were than women at everything as he greedily chomped down that delicious bar of "French" ex-lax. I was not privy to this scene but I wish I had seen and heard Tony bragging and munching while Donny and Linn Sue barely contained their laughter. I did, however, witness, via my olfactory nerves, the aftermath when I went into the bathroom. Tony sat on the toilet for six hours, from 4:00 p.m. to 10:00 p.m. He missed his favorite sporting event—dinner. After that, no more stupid tricks were played by anyone. We were now all able to concentrate on being crazy again.

    I continued to play a lot of pool and I continued to succeed at it. I was still amped up pretty good and when I was in this state I played high speed, aggressive pool and made most of my shots. Unfortunately, when the manic came down, so did my ability as a pool hustler. But while I was high, I was great!

    The person I played with most, of course, was Linn Sue. She was my best friend on the ward. There is a lot to be said about instant connection with a person. We did not know each other for a long period of time but it felt as if we had known each other all each other's lives. I was fortunate to have someone like that at such a desperate time. We talked about everything under the sun and bared our true feelings on just about every subject. Neither of us were angels, but both of us were a hell of a sight better than our wild behavior displayed at times. We were the co-record holders for being restrained and we were still kind, just, decent people. I loved her. She was as close to me as any guy friend I've had. It was weird, and it was special.

Chapter Fourteen

Immediately I was given a drug known as Lithobid which was a slow releasing tablet of Lithium Carbonate, the most effective mood regulator used to control bipolar affective disorder or manic depression (a title some of us non progressive lunatics like to cling onto because the initials M.D. makes us feel "cool").

For a week following the commencement of the Lithobid treatment, I was still in outer space trying to snort the fumes off of Will Robinson's jet pack. But then after about ten days, the medicine took a strangle hold of all my delusions and hallucinations. It was truly, truly amazing. I was sane and lucid again and coherent to anyone who spoke to me or questioned me. I was back. This of course meant that I was to be hospitalized for another two months while being completely sane. They wanted to do some fine tuning with me and continue on with the therapy to make sure that I was 100% well before I left the hospital. I could understand this and appreciate their concern, but waiting more than eight minutes to be released from a mental hospital sucks.

It was an interesting two months. Although I still needed therapy and my meds to be adjusted, for the most part I became an observer and student of mental illness. Hands on experience as I became confidant to some of the more deeply disturbed individuals on the ward. My main problem, after being properly medicated, was dealing with all the crazy things that I said and did. Most of the others were really screwed up compared to the post Lithium version of me. So, because I cared about these more disturbed individuals, I took it upon myself to be confidant. The perfect example of this was my relationship with Rich the schizophrenic. He was disliked by the others because he was so different and they nastily called him slug because when he was in his low affect phase, he did absolutely nothing but sit in a chair with an afghan draped over him—even if it was warm. I caught him on one of his more up days and developed a rapport. We had something in common immediately. He had some cassette tapes with him and his favorite was "Live Rust" by my Neil Young. I can still see old two hundred pound Rich jumping up and down singing "Cinnamon Girl" with enormous enthusiasm —I'll go so far as to say that this sixteen year old had more enthusiasm for the music of Neil Young than a child under the tree early Christmas morning. He couldn't sing worth shit and neither could I but we'd belt out the tunes on that album until we were told by popular demand to kindly shut up. But we never did, we just lowered the boom box a little, lowered our voices or moved to another vacant room. Alright, I'll admit the guy was a little weird, but he had phases when he was really quite intelligent, coherent and cool. I liked him despite what the others thought and found him to be quite interesting most of the time. He had been hospitalized four times prior and even spent some time at the hospital in Minnesota where the MMPI test was devised. Nobody knew what the hell to do with this guy and whenever his parents came to visit, the father and Rich would wind up in these horrific screaming matches over absolutely, positively nothing. Thus, the prognosis for Rich was bleak at very best. The meds he took were many, varied and powerful, but they didn't seem to do the trick. Therapy was useless for him also because he was smart enough to know that no matter how much talking is done, his problem was biogenic in nature and he'd suffer anyway. I felt tremendously sorry for him and just tried to listen to his stories so that he'd feel better but I don't think anybody could've helped him at that time. He was one of the patients that was there before and after my entire stint and on the day I left, I went to say goodbye to him and he was in a low affect phase and didn't even acknowledge my farewell. I often wonder what happened to him.

Another person who was pretty much out of it was Chang Le who was discharged only a couple of weeks after I was admitted. I'd sit on the couch and try to listen to her as she spoke but with her thick accent it was almost impossible to understand her and all I did was nod my head and way "yes" the whole time. I was also a little leery of her because of the incident where she grabbed my crotch. She was always smiling at me and I always felt that she was going to lunge at me at any moment but I was successful in always keeping her at an arms distance. She was another very interesting person. Her I could see getting better because I think she was just suffering from culture shock . . . she wasn't American, she was probably lonely and definitely libidinous. I suppose that could cause mental problems.

The others in the crowd were your average ordinary adolescents with one twist or another. As I had said earlier, it was drugs that sent a lot of these kids to the hospital. Many people thought I was on PCP when I blasted into the ranks. PCP, i.e. angel dust, was a prevalent drug in the late seventies and early eighties (I'm sure you can find it today, but I wouldn't know since I don't do it). The drug was the Superman drug giving plenty of energy to those who over-do-it. It surprised me when I found out that drugs was my first diagnosis. I found this out many weeks later in the schoolroom as I was just mulling through the folder that teacher Bob Edmonds had compiled on my education history. The top sheet of paper was a loose leaf note that had "ARCHIE MCRAE PCP ABUSER" scrawled in bold, thick, black magic marker. I stood, completely stunned for a good five minutes as I stared at this introduction. This was, after all, the first thing Bob and Harley (the other teacher) must have seen. This truly enraged me. I've never liked it when people tell me who or what I am, but putting down that I was PCP abuser on what I thought was my permanent record was almost enough to make me start throwing punches. Of course, this quick trigger temper in this state and all my energy was exactly why they thought I was a PCP abuser. Nonetheless, they should have thrown that sheet out when they had found out the doctor had diagnosed me with Manic Depression. I confronted Bob on this error, almost in tears. Bob was a great dude . . . very smart . . . very nice . . . very gentle and very patient. He was surprisingly sensitive for such a large burly man and he was a father type figure to us.

"Bob," my hand was shaking as I held the sheet, "you think I'm a PCP addict?" He looked at the sheet in my hand and quickly tried to pass off the subject by saying, "Oh that, that's nothing Arch, don't worry about it." Whenever somebody tells me not to worry about something, that's when I start doing my best worrying. I pressed the issue . . . "Wait a minute Bob. You mean to tell me everyone thought I was a drug addict?"

"Well, Arch, you were acting very strangely and your symptoms were similar to someone taking dust. It shouldn't alarm you that people thought you were under the influence because it's a very rare thing for someone to act the way you did naturally. You were the most energetic patient I've seen on this ward except for the possible exception of Linn Sue," he paused reflectively, "I'd give the nod to you because you're a better fighter. Believe me, the reason people thought you were on drugs is because nobody would imagine a good kid like you to suffer from a mental illness. It was too much of a shock for everyone, so they thought somebody had slipped you some serious drugs as a lark." This made an awful lot of sense and I checked my parents out on it. They said that was exactly what happened . . . so everyone got to live this turn around. They truly were inches from feeling the wrath of Archie McRae but as usual I was persuaded to compliance by someone who actually made sense.

NOTE: The thought of drugs made me wonder what I'd be like if I had actually taken an inordinate amount of drugs. The question becomes would I have survived a serious drug trip as well as a serious manic high at the same time? That's a very scary question. What's even scarier is thinking about people who have had undiagnosed manic depression and drug problems all their adult lives. My condition might not have been diagnosed had I been a loady. Fortunately, they went through my family history and found an abnormally high rate of alcoholism on both sides of the family. And it was well known over the years that manic depression and unipolar depression is often times masked by alcoholism.

Alcohol and other drugs mask the problem by inducing similar symptoms. If a person takes barbituates and is distraught it appears as if the person is in the depressed phase. If the person is on PCP or cocaine it can make it look as if the person is in the manic state. And of course the reason the manic depressive is taking the drug to begin with is to self medicate. When a manic is too high, he needs something to bring him down. When he is down he needs something to bring him up. Drugs . . . Drugs . . . Drugs! It's not a moral issue like we were taught when we were kids. It's not what's good or bad or right or wrong, it's simply what kills the pain. And the beauty of alcohol is that it's the only drug that does both . . . when you're down, a couple of drinks will anesthetize you, kill the pain and give you a buzz enough to forget your problems and make you feel "good." When you are as high as a kite and don't have a fistful of barbituates getting loaded on alcohol will fit the bill. Needless to say this is a dangerous and addictive way to kill your pain and it will eventually lead to self destruction. But it works for the time being. The question I postulate now is this, "Is excessive use of alcohol and drugs a moral issue when there is no seemingly other way to kill the pain that consumes the taker?" That's certainly something to consider the next time you call somebody a junky. Maybe they have underlying psychological problems that prevent them from being as perfect as you.

Needless to say, many manic depressives go through their entire lives without ever being diagnosed. Sometimes this is good, however, because the person doesn't have to go through life thinking of themselves as a "freak" or "nut."

I was fortunate to be caught and labeled in many respects. In many respects I was unlucky. After all, what sixteen year old boy would like to walk through his life with the label "manic depressive" tattooed to his forehead? I was grateful that I was diagnosed and being helped medically but on the flip side, I felt like a freak. I was sixteen and my identity as an adult was just being formed. I didn't like being classified with the mentally ill—can you blame me?

Chapter Fifteen

I'd be sorely remiss if I were to not take time and write about the last topic I discussed at the end of the last chapter—identity. This topic is hands down the single most important topic a manic must deal with except for how the disease makes you feel. Whether you like it or not, in order for you to recover from the illness, you must admit that, yes you are, mentally ill. Every time you take your medicine, which you have to do everyday, you are reminded that you are a manic depressive. Many times you won't be thinking about it when you take the medicine, but believe me, you never forget why you're on medicine. Whether it's conscious at the time is immaterial, the diagnosis or label, becomes a very real part of you that you cannot separate yourself from. Most people, including doctors will label you, all of you, as being Manic Depressives rather than an individual who suffers from the illness, Manic Depression. You and the illness are decreed inseparable and every day of your life you must bear the brunt of your illness and the stigma therefore attached to your label.

There are an estimated 2.4 million manic-depressives in the United States of America which populates an estimated 240 million citizens. This works out to be 1% of the population or 1 out of every 100 people. Many of these manic-depressives are in asylums or hospitals, many are on disability and don't go out much, many are in partial hospital programs, etc . . . etc. So it's reasonable to say that there are not many manics out there and you're a member of a minority much like being another race. The main difference is that members of different races know who each other are and can empathize and bond immediately. Those who are mentally ill don't know when they encounter one another out in the real world and there is so much stigma to being "crazy" that they hide and protect the secret that they have a mental illness. This causes a tremendous feeling of loneliness, and often times the person may not have the means to acquire psychotherapy or can't get to support groups. Not only is it a painful disease, it's a lonely one. Most "normal" folks get tired of the manic bitching and moaning, and they don't understand what the manic's been through. So there becomes this "me against the world" sensibility that truly plagues a manic if he/she allows him/herself to become overly sensitive.

The stigma itself, is a brutal burden for the manic (or anyone else mentally ill) to bear. High self esteem is difficult to achieve when there are so many different negative ways to label someone who is ill or insane. First, let's rattle off a few real quick just to show how society views and labels people who are supposedly ill: NUT, LUNATIC, BOOB, WACKO, WEIRDO, LOONY, GOOFBALL, KOOK, ETC . . . ETC . . . I listed eight separate, colorful titles off the top of my head to euphemistically describe those who act differently in the throes of mental illness. There are as many, if not more, ways to describe mental hospitals or asylums. I'm not personally offended by these titles, pending upon who is using them. There are just certain people who you'd rather not label you. But no matter who is labeling you, how politely, or why, it becomes very apparent that you are to be considered differently and sometimes the effect is negative and can cause damage to your self image. Your identity is scarred, whether you like it or not, the first time you're diagnosed.

I'm not suggesting that the mentally ill falter or crumble every time they are called a name or hear bad things about mental illness. I'm merely pointing out that there is a gross prejudice in society and it doesn't take the most astute "nut" in the world to realize the negative backlash is directed straight at him. This is what causes secrecy in the mentally ill. Most people hide their illness, particularly in the work world. Who would you pick for a job if two candidates were equal—the one who was or wasn't ill? So, the mentally ill find it necessary to hide a major part of their identity. It is not healthy for people to have to hide things that realistically should be globally accepted by modern society. Every once in a while I want to be able to stand up on a table in a busy restaurant, buck naked, and scream at the top of my lungs, "I suffer from manic depression and still am a wonderful human being!!! As a matter of fact, I might be better than all of you because I've had to suffer from your prejudice!!!" I'll be back in twenty minutes, it's dinner time and I have to go to the diner for dinner.

Alright, I'm back from jail now and I want to now discuss what results when a person suffers from stigma. As was mentioned earlier, self esteem is naturally lowered and this causes less confidence in oneself and very importantly, motivation is lowered. If a person thinks they're worthless, they will assume they can't do a lot of tasks they really can do. They won't even attempt a lot of things because they are convinced they are not worthy. This is a direct repercussion of the negative prejudice that society foists upon the mentally ill.

In many of the halfway houses or Community Living Arrangements that manics and other mentally ill people reside in, there is a staff of workers who'll do all the work and often times insist on doing the work for the "ill" client. This, of course, perpetuates the myth that the mentally ill are incapable of being worthy members of society. Thus, they learn helplessness, expect nothing of themselves, look forward to an unmotivated life, actually become dependent on other people, and most importantly perpetuate the negative stereotypes that are thrust upon them. This is the vicious cycle of the mentally ill. This is why, if the mentally ill play into the stereotypes, they will become what they're afraid of in the first place. If somebody tells you that you are unworthy and then does everything for you with a smirk on their face, you're sure in the hell going to feel worthless and then act accordingly. Logic. There is a good chance you are going to wind up with a king complex. Why help yourself when someone is being paid to help you? You are now royalty. Royalty with no self esteem.

The question then becomes, "Is there a resolution to this never ending identity crisis?" Certainly different forms of therapy and support groups help, but the most important weapon you can possibly have (in my opinion) is heart. You have to keep trying every day, no matter how hard that can be. You must brush aside the past and get on with your life, day in and day out. I have done well in the past, and I have failed miserably, but I'm still here trying. Every day is a new day and if you do what you can, your identity will strengthen. No matter what anyone says and even if you don't win the societal brass ring, you will be a winner. It is impossible to lose if you try. Trying is by definition, winning.

Chapter Sixteen

One of the breaks afforded me just after my second week was the permanent arrival of my sister Marty (Martha), a woman who I loved very deeply and passionately. Growing up, I often times thought she hated me because she used to pick fights with me for no reason, and me being much smaller than her, she'd win every fight. I cannot blame her for fighting me the way she did because I understand full well her circumstance. She had to deal with the issue of being an adopted child and growing up in a divorced family. She was also a high energy (quite hyperactive) individual who was by nature irrepressible. So whenever she had a bad day, I was there to be tortured. That was my job and I did it well. Of course, I was a hyper little man that probably deserve a good hit or two now and then just to keep me honest. I remember when I was five or six, Marty and I would have sword fights in the kitchen with the butcher knives while my mother was briefly at the store or something. This sort of lunacy was common place and I can't for the life of me figure out how we never got hurt. The fights were incessant but I always knew that Marty loved me to death, at least as much as how much I looked up to her. She is the person who taught me how to stick up for myself and put up a fight if there was anybody trying to start up with me, she'd offer her assistance, expertise and services. This is exactly what caused me to learn to fight for myself. There was no way I was ever going to let a girl, particularly my sister, put up a fight for me. Yes, it was nice and sweet of her to want to kick the crap out of my friends; no it was not going to happen. I fought.

This relationship I had with Marty was truly amazing. It was probably the first love-hate relationship I've ever experienced and the end result was that we were probably the closest two in the family. It's odd how the relationships you least expect to be healthy, may in fact turn out to be the healthiest in the long run. As an outsider, if you saw the two of us interact just once, you'd swear that we were mortal enemies and would never grow up to be friendly at all. The exact opposite was true and the reason became clear to me as time wore on—my sister Marty and I were truly brother and sister. We didn't need to be swimming in the same gene pool to know this. We played hard, we fought hard, we laughed hard, we loved hard.

It was not my intention to welcome Marty back to California while behind lock and key of a mental hospital. In fact, I was deeply ashamed and embarrassed. I was the fair haired child. Why was this happening to me and what would my big sister think? With Kim, she came down the corridor wearing blue jeans, a black blouse, a white blazer, and the palest face I've ever seen in my life. The first words out of my mouth were not, "Hi Marty. How are you doing?" The first words were, "What's wrong with you pale face?" She didn't know what to think of that greeting coming from her normal brother who was now supposedly psychotic. She looked in awe as she hugged me hard and kissed me. "What kind of greeting is that bro?" I just laughed, kissed her and showed her to a comfortable blue rubber chair in one of the back greeting rooms. Kim, of course tagged along silently. Kim can be very quiet at times. I can't say that I blame her, being the middle child sandwiched between the king and the queen of adrenalin. "What's wrong Marty, I've never seen you this pale before, are you sick or something?" She brushed this inquiry aside, "No, Archie, I'm fine." There were tears welling in her eyes, "I'm here to see if you're alright." I was truly appreciative of her concern, but if there is anything I hate, it's when someone asks me if I'm alright. It reminds me that I'm sick. You see, I have a tremendous ability of being able to forget that I'm sick. Combined with my high threshold of pain, this can be a deadly combination. When I was ten and had a sledding accident and ruptured my spleen, after several hours, I was taken to the hospital and literally almost bled to death waiting for a doctor because the intake people thought I only had a bruise. They later told my mother that there was no way I should have been walking with the condition my removed spleen was in. This is why I can't stand being asked how I'm doing . . . I've already found my own way of denying the sickness. One more case in point was in junior high school when I was on an ice hockey team. I was constantly sick with the flu but still managed to make it to school, games and practice. Simple denial and high energy level.

"Why does everybody keep asking me how I'm doing when all I want to do is go home?"

I spoke softly as Marty softly rebutted.

"Archie, you're not well. It's going to take time to straighten you out." My sister Martha never pulled punches with me. When she spoke seriously I listened. I didn't always agree, but I listened. "But . . . ?" I stammer as she interjected quickly, "No buts Archie," she pointed at me, "you behave yourself in here and do what the doctors and nurses say . . . no complaining, no bullshit . . . you behave yourself and then you can come home."

I did not speak for quite some time. It was good to see Marty, but she wasn't saying exactly what I wanted to hear. I have two reactions when I'm mad . . . when on a manic edge I lash out . . . other times bring silence. This time I just sat there a touch hurt and dumbstruck. She was starting all over again, she just came from three thousand miles away to boss me around. I was looking down at the floor when my sister Kim chimed in, "Archie? Aren't you even going to ask her how she's doing? You haven't seen her in months."

"I'm sorry, how ya doing Mart?"

"Fine Arch, it's good to get out of Darby . . . that place starts to get depressing when it's cold." She was right about that one.

"How's dad?"

"You tell me Arch . . . You called him the other day, yelled at him for no good reason and then hung up . . . since when are you a cheap shot artist?"

She was right again and again I grew quiet and looked at the floor for a moment, "I know, I'm sorry."

"Don't apologize to me Archie, apologize to Dad . . . you hurt him for no reason."

She was right and I did apologize to Dad later that night. Whenever my father and I fight, the one who is being a jerk usually apologizes shortly thereafter. This time it was my turn.

I still couldn't get over how pale Marty was and I commented on it once again, "Why do you look so pale? Are you alright?"

She seemed annoyed by this, "Archie, will you please stop asking me that? I'm fine."

"See, you don't like it either. It sucks when people keep asking you how you're doing."

"Alright, alright Archie. I won't ask that anymore."

"Okay," finally I was happy. "Hey Marty, you know what I was thinking, why don't you and me form a stand-up act together and become comedians. We're the funniest people I know. We'll make millions of dollars." She didn't seem too keen on the idea.

"I'm not a comedian Archie," she was lying. Some of the best laughs I ever had were with her.

"Ah, come on, it'll be fun," I was pleading like a child.

"Archie," she paused. "I can't speak in public."

"I'm telling you, we'll make millions," a gleam came to my eye, "all you have to do is say yes, and we'll go right to work on an act."

"No, I don't think so Arch," she paused and then changed the subject. "How do you like the other kids?"

"They're nuts."

"I saw a couple of cute girls, if I know you, you're loving that." She was right, she knew her little brother alright.

"Yea, they're alright I guess." I'm always a little leery of giving Marty information on what girl I like. This fear stems from when I was in the third grade and Marty found out I had a crush on my cute little classmate Pam Dawson and kept screaming "Archie and Pammy Dawson!!! Archie and Pammy Dawson!!!" in a sing-song manner every time she stepped foot in our side of the building. It was the most embarrassing thing that happened to me to date. It was worse than the time Jenny Dobbs kissed me when I was in kindergarten. On the way home from school one day, Jenny gave me a quick kiss when we parted and unbeknownst to me; my loving, adorable, passive sister was walking right behind me. The remaining four block walk home I heard a resounding chorus of "Archie kissed a girl!!! Archie kissed a girl!!!" This is probably why, to this day, I cannot ask a woman out on a date. Come to think of it, I think I'll get on a plane and go knock her out for those fond memories. But, I'll give her one thing, she is funny.

"Which one are you hot for?" She got up and walked out into the TV room and looked around all nosy like. I, of course, sat in the back room with my face in my hands, mentally preparing myself for a fresh onslaught of poking from my inimitable sister Martha.

A minute later Martha came back with a huge grin on her face. "Okay Kim there's three girls out there, all of them good looking . . . One of them is a six foot red head. One of them is an average size blonde and the last is a short China girl. Which do you think bro is pining for?"

Kim, who was obviously uncomfortable in the place, nonetheless pitched in . . . "Well, traditionally Archie's not into blondes and a six foot red head would be like him climbing Mount Everest when it's on fire. So I'll vote for the China doll." Good ole Kim, quietly both smart and funny.

"Ah c'mon, Archie and a China doll, never." At that precise instant, I made a fatal mistake—I smiled. Marty looked stunned, flabbergasted even, "You mean? . . . You mean you like . . ." she paused to gain her composure. "Well this is new. You've been in California too long, boy." And then as I feared she loudly let me have it in that back room, "Archie and the China doll!!! Archie and the China doll!!!!" If my adorable sister dies an unfortunate death of unnatural causes, you'd be wise not to rule me out. (This, of course, for those of you scoring at home, is a joke.)

My sisters only stayed about fifteen minutes or so which was the norm for my stay in the hospital. They'd drive half an hour each way just to say, "Hi! How are you doing?" and then go home. I can't say that I blame them or anything, the other kids had a tendency to display their version of adolescent egocentrism. They got louder, more boisterous, and downright rude at times.

A case in point, Donny and Bobby were having a catch with the nerf football and wouldn't stop when Kim was walking down the hallway. They almost hit her in the head which of course meant that I almost had to hit them in the head. Those bozos are lucky it wasn't Marty they almost hit. She'd turn around and stick that nerf up ole Bobby's left nostril. He'd have nerf foam coming out of his ears for a month. But because these less mature characters of the tribe acted up when my sisters showed, my sisters came briefly and then left. Like I said earlier, who can blame them for this brevity, after all, who wants to hang out in a "nut house?" I thank them for the frequency at which they did actually come.

That night at the pool table, Linn Sue was very bouncy and smiley and playful. I couldn't quite figure out what had gotten into her, so I just came right out and asked her. "What is wrong with you, girl? You keep acting like that and someone's going to lock you up." She continued to beam, staring right into my eyes and I frustratedly begged, "What?!" She laughed on the other side of the table and then really began to tease me. "I've got a secret!!! I've gotta secret!!! I've gotta secret!!!"

"Don't make me come over there, woman," I made a quick move to my left as she let out a scream. "You better tell me or it's lights out honey!" I was laughing pretty heavily there myself until the next sentence out of her beautiful mouth. "I'm going home Archie!!! I'm going home!" I've never seen a happier, more beautiful face in my life and all I could do was feel hurt. If I had a spleen in my body it would have exploded at this moment. Instead of feeling and sharing joy with my friend Linn Sue, I felt the loss and it showed on my distraught face.

"Archie? What's wrong?" She looked at me concerned. "I thought you'd be happy for me."

"Well yea, of course I'm happy for you." I sounded completely dejected.

"You don't sound too happy," she was earnest.

"No, I am happy for you," I looked down as I paused, "but you're my best friend in here. What am I supposed to do without you?" I was almost in tears.

"Archie?!" She pleaded. "Look at me." I couldn't look up at her, as if I were a wounded child. "You're the greatest!!" I knew she meant it. "You'll be fine without me. You'll be strong. I haven't known you long but I know a caliber man when I see one," she paused, "Archie, please, please, look at me." I couldn't. "Archie, please be happy for me. It means a lot to me." She then walked away from me.

Later that night, after my shower, I went out of my way to apologize to my friend. I truly was very happy for her. But in that short span of time, I had managed to fall in love with her, and displaying my contentment for her great news was overrided by the despair that rocked my young, labile, emotional world.

But I understood my mistake and set forth to correct the situation. I met up with Linn Sue in the school. She was reading a magazine and listening to the Doobie Brothers "Minute by Minute" album which was sort of the album and song appropriate to the ward.

I approached softly, "Linn Sue?" she did not look up at me. "Linn Sue? I just came to tell you that I'm sorry I didn't tell you how really happy I am that you're going home. I was being selfish. I mean, we just became friends and all and I don't want that to come to an end. So, I just thought I better apologize and wish you all the luck in the world because I truly mean it." She still didn't look up at me so I turned to leave the room.

"Are you gonna be an asshole all of your life or is this just a phase you're going through?" I started to laugh as I turned to look her in the eye. "I'm hoping that when I graduate from high school someone gives me a pound of tact as a graduation gift."

She smiled, "I'm gonna miss you too buddy," her eyes engaged mine, "but we still have two weeks, you know."

"Really," this news brought a rise out of me, "when's the date?"

"December 8th." She smiled.

THERE'S A DATE FOR YOU ROCK AND ROLL FANS—DECEMBER 8, 1980.

Around that time I was blessed with a roommate. He was little Dave the ultimate drug addict/diabetic. What a wonderful combination—can you say "coma?" I think you can. Anyway, ole Dave was a pretty good dude, considering the fact that he was incredibly cynical for someone thirteen years of age. Somehow this kid hated everybody—but in a truly hilarious way. There were only two things I disliked about this dude. One, he had the worst smelling foot odor known to man. It was so bad, I felt it down in the Vas Deferens (that one is for any med students reading). The second thing I couldn't stand about the kid was his taste in music. The name of the band was ACDC and he played that album "Back in Black" every damned night before he went to sleep. Three chords and some raspy voiced, deranged, knicker kneed Australian screaming the same words over and over and over again. Sweet dreams Archie. On the third night of this, I caught myself trying to kill the boy. My right hand just kept reaching and reaching for my buddy Dave's throat but my left hand reached out and stopped it, saving Dave's life. I fell to my knees and begged him to turn that crap off (crap is an opinion of course. A strong opinion, but an opinion nonetheless). He did not comply, so I grabbed him by the pajama tops, sat him straight up, looked him square in the eye and threatened his young life. This got the message across. He now knew, officially, that Archie McRae was not an ACDC fan. To this day, if I ever get stuck hearing that title song, you can see the demons dancing in my eyes as my ire rises to seize hold of my esophagus. Quite the transformation. Years later, when I'd be at dance clubs, they'd play that song and I'd literally race out of the building. That happened several times and all my buddies who I used to run with would get a big kick out of my shenanigans, but I was dead serious.

So me and Dave had some negotiating in the early stages of our roommate ship. All good partnerships start out with a scrape or two. Although I didn't appreciate his all out war on the world in general, I did respect the fact that every morning at six o'clock that kid was awake so that he put a needle in his arm to control his diabetes, an illness he had no control over nor asked for. It's a man who does what he has to, and I admired the fact that he'd just get out of bed at that hour without thinking about it.

Speaking of being a man, now is the time I get to tell you about Tony's last stand. Yee ha! Wait until you get a load of this one:

Once upon a time on the adolescent ward, there roamed a grease ball who for no apparent reason performed malicious acts on poor unsuspecting patients who deserved neither malice nor hardship of any kind. This patient, who we'll call (oh, let's see) Tony, would not only perform devious practical jokes but would also instigate vicious arguments for no reason whatsoever. Now, one fine morning when the entire staff and clientele was congregating in the TV room for the morning rounds, a loud argument was heard at the pool table and low and behold if it wasn't our hero Tony and client Bobby who was also quite the annoying piece of work but to a much lesser degree.

Well then, since the whole community was there, the muscle bound psyche techs, led by Cliff, the dude you'd least like to mess with, decided it appropriate to converge on the troubled area. Now, Bobby, being the victim in this scenario, raised his hands professing his innocence and ran around the pool table, down the hall, into the TV room and literally jumped into a rubber couch. This was, of course, substantial entertainment for the likes of Dave and myself, but it gets so much better.

Tony, who was cornered against the back wall of the ward, had grabbed a pool cue and was threatening to kill the psyche heads while everyone on the ward watched on, most of us rather amused.

"Any of you assholes come near me and I'll take your mother fucking heads off!" So spoke the thirteen year old with the stick in his hand. Since the psyche techs were trained to talk their patients down, they did just that, they tried to talk sense into Tony for five long minutes. During this time, three more psyche techs were called up and they assumed a position on the far side of the pool table. So, it was Tony against six psyche techs lined in a row right in front of him about ten feet away. All along the psyche techs tried to cajole Tony but he was so damned stubborn he just insisted on hitting someone if anybody came near. He then said something that I'll never forget, "I don't care if this is my last stand, you assholes aren't coming near!" Dave and I almost lost our bladders when we heard that one. Finally, one of the doctors gave the okay to restrain Clint Eastwood (normally the techs would have acted much faster, but since the doctors were around, they followed procedure to the T) and as they approached, Tony fooled us all by dropping the stick, sticking his head down and running full bore in between the techs as if he were a fullback running through the line. Clifford, who was a superlative athlete as I mentioned earlier, tackled this boy by the legs from behind, as two of the techs tried to hold down his upper body. Now, I paint an ugly portrait of Tony, but to his credit, he is strong as an ox and he fought tooth and nail with all his strength as all the techs grabbed every extremity until that wild animal lost his strength. It literally took ten staff members to subdue him in a period of time of about five minutes. That's a long time for that kind of struggle. Every one of us sat in awe watching this but Dave and I started laughing beyond control—Tony farted! I know, that's childish and disgusting on our part, but the bastard had it coming.

As time rolled on toward Linn Sue's discharge date, I spent as much time as possible with her. We talked about everything under the sun including her theory that in her next life she'd come back as a squirrel because she said she'll always feel the need to be around nuts. This was definitely my kind of girl. After the medicine kicked in and the delusions began to subside, I realized that Donna was not the girl for me and that Linn Sue was the girl I cared for. Unfortunately, the day she left was the last time I was to ever see her. I asked on numerous occasions for her home phone number, and each time she gave me the answer no. In way of explanation, she told me that she wanted to put the whole experience behind her and that if we were to continue on as friends in the outside world I would be bringing back bad old memories by association. I understood this way of thinking but I also understood the way I felt about this girl and how hard it was to let go of her. I argued vehemently that I would be a good support to her, knowing what she had been through and actually having shared the experience with her. This did not sell on any of the times I brought it up to her. She'd get annoyed and tell me that she'd miss me and always remember me, but that in no way shape or form were we to contact each other outside the hospital.

NOTE: Discharge time is a strange and exciting, as well as confusing, time. When Linn Sue told me about wanting to shove all her memories of the hospital under the carpet, I understood.

We all had our choices of staying in contact with others or to let go of the ties that we formed. I believe that most of us did not keep in contact with the others. I also believe that this decision is a regret for some of us. The desire to just have the whole damn thing over with was a valid well deserved reward for all of us.

So the big day came and I was forced to let go of a fantastic friend. I took it like a man but inside my young heart was broken in about a thousand pieces. Linn Sue, Julie, and myself sat in one of the back waiting rooms talking for a while and saying our last goodbyes when Rich came blasting in yelling frantically, "John Lennon's dead!!! John Lennon's dead!!!"

"What!?" I shot back at him figuring it was just a delusion of his.

"John Lennon was shot in New York! I'm not kidding!" I looked at Julie and Linn Sue and we all had stunned expressions and then all three of us ran out into the TV room. Six adolescents, all of whom were weaned and raised on rock and roll watched the news coverage with their jaws on the floor. Rich was right, John Lennon was dead and most rock and roll fans were simply appalled at the senseless way he died. He had a strong impact, not just on his generation, but the following few generations as well. As for us on the ward, we all stood silent until Julie sat down and started weeping. Linn Sue and I rallied around her and tried to console her but she balled her eyes out for quite some time. After several moments of all of us being dumbstruck by the news, reality decided to intervene. Cliff came up to us and softly spoke to Linn Sue, "I don't mean to interrupt you at a time like this, but your parents are here. They're waiting for you downstairs."

"Okay," she spoke softly and dejectedly as if she had been kicked in the stomach or as if she'd just lost her best friend. The latter might have been what was just about to happen to her. She began to cry as she went over and gave Julie a tight, long hug. Both young ladies were now weeping. This was too much for me, so I kind of roamed off down the corridor, feeling a tremendous sense of loss. I thought I would cry at this moment and I didn't want anyone to see me. I should have cried but never really did as I tried to be a "man" about the situation. I waited for her down by the front door and her and Cliff came about five minutes thereafter. Linn Sue was still crying and as sad looking as I remember seeing her. Oddly, she also looked more beautiful than I had ever seen her. It was the last time I was to see her. When she approached me she dropped the bag she was carrying and threw her arms around me, kissed my cheek and held me as tight as I had ever been held to that point in my life. She must have held me for a solid two minutes until Cliff prompted her, "Come on kiddo, it's time to go home," and then my friend let go and threatened me, "Listen Archie, you be good or I'll kick

the crap out of you in a future life." Promises. Promises.
 I had a hard time speaking to her, "Be good. Good luck and I'll miss you." I then kissed her hard on the cheek and watched Cliff escort her out the security doors. It took every ounce of restraint not to cry, but I didn't. Oh boy, I guess that made me a "man."

Chapter Seventeen

Meetings. Meetings. Meetings. Meetings. Meetings. Meetings. Meetings. Meetings. Meetings. Meetings. Meetings.
When you enter the hospital as a patient it is best for you to prepare yourself mentally for a deluge of meetings. Meetings in the mornings with the doctors, staff and patients. Meetings for individual therapy with your psychologist at least three times a week. Meetings with your psychiatrist concerning medications and other hully bully one time a week. Meetings with other patients in group therapy at least one time a week. Meetings at night twice a week with your family unit and a given social worker. Meetings at different kinds of training with the psyche techs twice a week (i.e. Assertion training geared to teach us how to act assertively rather than aggressively) etc. And then there was the big pooh bah meeting itself every Wednesday night from 7:00-9:00—the meeting where the whole community fills a large room downstairs. Every patient and their nuclear families (or anybody else related to the families that want to attend), the psyche techs on duty, a couple of social workers and a doctor or two, are the folks that gather to discuss how everyone is doing. Basically, this meeting was for both the families, particularly the parents, and the patients. It was for the parents and families because it kept these people abreast of what was going on with their loved ones in the hospital. It also gave the families a chance to meet the other families and other patients. Once a family member plays a part in this process, their fears and tensions are alleviated about the whole process and they, themselves, can make contributions to everyone by speaking out and giving advice, etc. In this way, they can give the whole community insight on their particular loved one and receive insight back from others. This is beneficial to themselves because they feel that they are playing a role in the progress of their child/sibling. And if they don't get anything out of it, they can have free donuts and coffee. Yippee!! The pooh Bag meeting was also beneficial to the patients because you could scope out the opposite sex members of all the families. As I recall, Donny had a sister my age with some mighty fine gamms. Wait a minute, that's not why it was beneficial to the patients. It was beneficial to the patients in that it gave us hope. It was nice seeing our

loved ones come out and support us in our time of need. They also provided a certain amount of normalcy. You looked like a family unit when together and that in itself was important. The more you think of yourself as "normal" the easier it was to bear the brunt of hospitalization. And then again, of course, there were donuts. Nothing like hyperactive, hormonal, adolescent mental patients with a sugar rush at 9:00 p.m. on a Wednesday night. Party. Party. Party.

The first of these big meetings I attended was when I was still high as a kite. I filed in with the rest of the patients and wound up not even sitting with my family but next to Roger, quite the cool patient, who had no family members in attendance. My parents were surprised by this but couldn't do anything about drawing me near as all the seats were rapidly obtained by everyone who rushed to find seating when the doors were opened. This first meeting was phenomenal as I began to get into one of those manic, comic, spins. Roger and Donny could not stop laughing for the first twenty minutes as I made wildly imaginative remarks (which, of course, I don't remember) under my breath. Finally, after awhile, people started to take notice of us laughing despite our attempts to keep the laughter as quiet as possible. Doctor Stewart turned to me and told me to be quiet and stop disrupting the group or I'd be escorted back to the ward. Well, I looked at my stepfather, and he was not pleased. I looked at my mother and she had a grimace/frown on her face that I saw only a few times on my mother's face. It meant that I was in for it if she ever got a hold of me. So, since I was in a very labile state, my jocularity immediately turned to shame, hurt, disgust, self loathing and embarrassment. I was in that sensitive frame of mind and affect. I did not say another word and barely held back my tears the remaining hour and a half. Afterwards, my parents said nothing because they realized by the way I was moping that I was already torturing myself for being bad. They know me well enough and realize when I'm being hard on myself.

The other most memorable big meeting was a couple of weeks after Marty came back to California. By this time I had been home a couple of times on passes and on this one particular occasion Marty and I had been clowning around and we were playing at the typewriter and she said she'd teach me how to use the typewriter. Well, she taught me by teaching me the same sentence ten times in a row, "Archie McRae is a jerk!" We didn't pay much attention to this Tom Foolery and we left the paper in the typewriter. Later that week, my stepfather found this piece of paper and it prompted him to bring this up in the big meeting. Dr. Stewart was focusing on me in the very beginning of this particular meeting, and I was pretty high and happy and told him that I was feeling great and no problems existed. My

stepfather then asked (in front of forty people) "Archie, I hear you when you say you're doing okay, but why did I see 'Archie McRae is a jerk' all over a paper you left in the typewriter?"
 Well, maybe it was my delivery, but everyone burst into laughter when I militantly pointed at Martha and said, "I didn't write that, she did!" Business as usual with ole sis and I.
 I had no problem with any of the meetings, as I usually got some idea or thought of worth out of them. The meetings most beneficial to me were the individual therapy sessions. As I had mentioned earlier, there was a tremendous feeling of freedom and the confidentiality aspect was an enormous bonus. Even if you can trust a friend to talk to, there still may be the chance that this friend may let your secrets slip by mistake. The therapist doesn't usually know your friends and it wouldn't matter if they did let something slip; which I'm sure they don't anyway.
 My next favorite meetings were the group therapy sessions with one therapist, one psyche tech and approximately eight patients. It was quite interesting hearing what people my own age had to say about life in general. It amazed me that each one of us were so drastically different yet so ultimately alike. The first thing we had in common was the fact that we were stuck behind the big glass doors with the wire running through the glass. The next thing we all had in common was some kind of problem fitting into the outside world. This is what the group therapy was all about—discussing all of the problems that kept us from functioning "normally" in society. Many a tear was shed in this group and the binds that held us together as a unit were strengthened with each revelation of fear and joy. I always enjoyed the group because there was no playing around. This is where we truly revealed ourselves and the statements that we made about life and the human condition were often times incredibly profound and inspired. Being a "punk" adolescent or a "crazy" person is enough impetus for a "normal" adult to immediately dismiss what comes out of the crazy punk's mouth. Right? . . . wrong! Words of wisdom would reverberate in that closet sized room whenever we met. Some of the sanest things that were ever said to me came out of the mouths of people that were supposedly insane. Does that make sense? Could it possibly be that some of us who are mentally ill are actually saner or more advanced than those who are considered normal? Is our difference a threat to them?
 Another meeting we had once a week was a family meeting with a social worker. This meeting truly sucked. For one thing, it was after everybody's work and everyone was blatantly exhausted. Second, Mr. Daniels, the social worker, made my mother out to be the scapegoat by suggesting that she raised me wrong. He said this to her when my mother was giving him the

family history. Well, Mom told me this and I was genuinely pissed off. My mother raised the three of us right and no bozo with letters behind his name was going to convince me otherwise. His credibility with me was shot before the first family meeting. He asked a lot of probing questions about this, that and the other thing, but he really found no concrete evidence suggesting that it was my upbringing or environment that caused my illness. The answer was simple, I have a biochemical imbalance in my brain that will never go away but can be controlled to a certain extent with no guarantee that there will be no further relapses. So this meeting didn't do much for me, mostly because I didn't like the man leading the group. As for how much it did for my family, I'm not at liberty to say. They must have taken some stock in it because we had two or three weekly meetings after I was out of the hospital and at home. But that didn't last as we all just went about our lives. At that point in time it was evident that I was back on the normy trail.

One thing I did get out of those family meetings was that you can have your master's degree in social work, have a lofty, high paying position and still be an uncaring, incompetent, rude, moron. That's what I learned from him. I figured there was hope for mankind yet if he could succeed.

Chapter Eighteen

Approximately a week after Marty's arrival I was allowed to go home on the weekends on either six or twelve hour passes. If you had no infractions on the board, and you received written permission from your doctor, then you could have two days of twelve hour passes on Saturdays and Sundays only. If you had one infraction on the board, then you could have two six hour passes with permission from your doctor. I had calmed down from my frenetic first two weeks substantially and the infraction board was free from the two words it had previously loved most—Archie McRae.

Of course, during the days when sprung from the pokey, the great Arch had to play a little ball with some of his old buddies at Murdy Park. Apparently the great Arch was missed by one and all and every one wanted the great Arch on their team. They had missed the maniacal midget point guard and his stellar leadership. That shot from the stratosphere that hit nothing but net. Those crisp, clean, sharp passes that poets down at Huntington Beach are still writing about. Their lyrical verses also encompass the thievery of the great Arch late in the tightest of games and the ubiquitous, adhesive man to man coverage that caused mucho, mucho, distress for the hombres mas grande que Archie. They also scroll about how the great Arch is a martyr playing for naught seeing as the babes only watch basketball in the gym. Ah yes, those poets and lyricists, ah yes.

The second weekend I was back, I was called by my old buddy Hasseim and asked to come to his residence. So I did . . . and whamo! Lo and behold! At least twenty of my friends from Model United Nations screaming "Surprise!!!" Well to be quite frank, I had never been so embarrassed and humiliated in all my young life. Come to think of it, I don't think I've been so embarrassed or humiliated to this date. A party for me and all I had to do was have a death defying nervous breakdown to get it. Wee hee!! I guess they all thought that since during my delusional time all I did was talk about a party then that's what would make me feel better—a party. They didn't seem to realize that having a party for me, albeit nice, was kind of like throwing salt into my wounds. The party was like throwing back all my delusional cockiness in my face only a month after I had made a fool of myself and spawned my lifelong reputation as a "weirdo."

    I stood on the stoop with my heart in my mouth wanting to run when I saw a very, very good looking Gina Daniels rapidly approaching the door with both arms extended, sweetly shrilling, "Archie!!!" She ran onto the stoop and strangled my stunned body with her beautiful arms and kissed my frozen face to excess. My heart was about to explode for three different reasons. First, my heart was about to burst due to the shock of the surprise itself. Second, the embarrassment and humiliation, coupled with the anger that goes along with it, was enough to kill me. And then, if that wasn't enough, this beautiful girl that most guys my age would die for, was kissing my face off. Whoa baby! Forget the embarrassment, forget the humiliation. Long live lust!!! Or as some of my amigos south of the border say, "Viva el lusto Sparky!!!" This girl was flat out gorgeous and under normal circumstances would not give me so much as a look. When my astonishment was eased a bit, the first thing I thought was, "I gotta have more nervous breakdowns!" Then this fine young lady took my hand and led me through the doorway where I was greeted by three other girls equally as notable as Gina. They literally waited in line to hug and kiss me. I couldn't believe it, I thought, "Hell, forget being a rock star, this mental illness deal gets the babes just as well." And on top of this, every one of those girls, who were all my friends, took it upon themselves to dress immaculately as if they were on a date. My trepidation about entering the party, as well as my feelings of being a weirdo, rapidly melted, I was truly amongst friends.

    The guys at the party were also glad to see me but none of them, not one of them, kissed me or dressed as if they were on a date. Go figure. All those lose bags said were, "yea, yea Arch, good to see you, let's go play ping pong." Since they didn't extend the courtesy of sprucing up for the return of the great Arch, they had to pay. I mopped the floor with all of them for two hours with the fervor and delight of an impish manic on leave.

    I was wrought with mixed emotions the whole time I was at this party. On the positive side, it was sweet of my friends to do this for me and it was particularly nice of them to give me a party which I was begging for on my manic high. They literally gave me what I was screaming for but I didn't want it the way I got it. I detected a touch of pity on the part of some of the guests and that part I truly despised. I'm not to be pitied or a recipient of charity. Exclamation point! Chandra (Hasseim's sister who was my age—and a friend of mine) and her mother were the biggest culprits of this pitying onslaught, but I couldn't express my anger towards these two because they were throwing the party and their intentions were solid and good. The reason I was so mad at these two, more than anybody else, was because the mother (a teacher at our school), took it upon herself to tell all of my teachers at my school that I was at a mental hospital and would be until further notice, and Chandra, who was a friend of Donna Seznick, took it upon *herself* to tell Donna Seznick, who I hardly knew, all the things I had said in the neighborhood and that I was in a hospital. Well, I was too confused by all the attention and excitement and really made no kind of rebuttal when confronted by these news flashes. When in a normal state and something angers me, I have a tendency to whip out the salt, sprinkle it and then eat my anger. Yum! Yum! The good little boy syndrome prevailed once again.

On my walk back home, just before the trip to the hospital. I thought about how terrible it must have felt for Donna Seznick to hear all of that crap about me marrying her and all. The poor girl must have thought that I was a stalker. My first resolution was to call this girl on my next pass home and apologize profusely until my ears bled. And that is exactly what I did, on the next Saturday, early in the day, I sucked up sixteen years of courage and called the young lady:

"Hello," I sheepishly spoke, "is Donna in?"

"Yes, one moment please, I'll get her," that must have been her mother. She sounded sweet, but I was in this tunnel of angst, a place I frequent whenever I speak to a beautiful woman. And then came the sweet sound of one of the friendliest, perkiest voices ever given an angel by God himself.

"Hello?" I froze like a bison in the Tundra and Donna was forced to ask again, only this time more inquisitively. "*Hello?*" the pause was unbearable, but before the young lady hung up on me, I blurbed out a very healthy, "Uhhhh?"

"Who is this?" I started to pace the kitchen floor anxiously, which is my trademark when making an idiot out of myself to young lady acquaintances over the phone. She was just about to hang up when I blasted, "Please don't hang up! . . . it's uh, Archie McRae?" I flinched when I spoke my own name.

"Are you sure?" she laughed heartily.

"Yea, I think so, just let me catch my breath before I have a seizure," and I did just that, I took a deep breath and jumped back into the fire.

"Yes, my name is Archie McRae and I'm calling to apologize to you."

"First of all, Archie, relax—BREATHE!" she paused, "second, why are you apologizing to me?"

"Well, I uh . . ." I couldn't think.

"Archie? Are you okay?" She was genuinely concerned which made my heart skip a beat. Man, God blessed me with an ability to spot women with class. That's one talent I know I have for sure.

"Yea, I guess I'm doing alright," I was sweating, "Chandra

told me that she talked to you."

"Yea, I'm really sorry to hear about your sickness."

"Oh, yea it's no big deal," NO BIG DEAL!!! "But that's not why I'm calling. I'm calling to apologize for saying all of those things about marrying you and all. I was really messed up I guess."

"Oh, that's okay, it was kind of flattering in a weird way. I just hope you're okay because you're really a nice guy," this chick truly was this cool.

"Yea, I'm doing good," there was a relaxed pause for a moment and as naturally and gracefully as I had ever done in my life, I said, "Would you like to go go out and do something with me today?"

"You know I have a boyfriend don't you?" Yes, I knew she had a boyfriend. While in the manic state, it just slipped my mind. Poof!!! Hey, you can't remember everything when you're completely insane. (She was dating a senior who was a straight "A" student, accepted at West Point, and the starting off guard for the varsity basketball team. 6'1", good looking—you know, the guy you want to accidentally run over 47 times in the parking lot of the local supermarket while he's helping an old lady carry her cookies to her car).

"Yea, you're going out with Chuck Townshend," I didn't put a lot of heart behind that statement. I then paused, "I mean, you know, go out as friends."

"Oh, sure, why not, I don't have anything to do today, what do you want to do?"

"I don't know, how about bowling?"

"Sure, I've been wanting to do that for some time," she sounded excited about the prospect. "When will you pick me up?"

"Oh," I sounded dejected, "I can't drive yet, I mean my parents won't let me yet, I sort of stole my mom's car when I was sick. I should be driving by 1990."

She laughed appropriately, "Well then, I'll drive."

"Okay. Cool. When do you want to go?"

"How about one?"

"That would be nice," I was smiling and relaxed. "I'll walk over to your house at one."

"You sure you know where it is?" she laughed.

"Ha, ha . . . how was I to know that your street was cut in half by a green house. What kind of street is cut in half by a greenhouse?"

She laughed again, "Well then, I'll see you at one buddy."

A friendship was born.

When I knocked on Donna's door, I was understandably nervous once again but I was greeted by a wonderful woman who turned out to be her mother. Her mom was gregarious, amiable and had the same sense of humor as Donna. I spoke to her for a couple of moments and she brought me a glass of iced tea as I waited for Donna to finish getting ready. After a few moments of pleasantries and a few good laughs, she felt comfortable with me enough to bring up the topic of my illness and I really didn't mind:

"I understand you've had a rough time lately."

"Oh, yes ma'am." I looked at my shoes.

"You know, Donna's grandfather was diagnosed manic depressive."

"Oh, really," I sounded interested.

"Yes, he takes that medicine. The wonder drug." She yelled up to Donna, "What's that drug Grandpa's taking?"

"Lithium!" she yelled. "Archie, I'll be right down!"

"Yes, that's the name . . . Lithium," she grabbed my wrist as she smiled, "is that what you are taking?"

"Yes ma'am, that and Navane," I looked up at her, square in the eye and serious.

"Oh dear," she put her hand on my shoulder, "don't be alarmed or scared or anything, that drug is the best thing that ever happened to my father-in-law. Yea, his life has straightened out entirely, and he's even nicer and sharper than ever. A smart nice young man like you, you'll have no problems. Donna thinks you're real nice and smart and she's always been a good judge of character. Just be sure to take your medicine." I smiled at her with genuine affect. I was thinking she was nice when her exuberant casually dressed daughter bounded down the stairs.

"Hi Archie," she smiled the smile around which my massive crush was developed.

"Ready to get your butt kicked in bowling?" I couldn't believe how nice these people were. I thought they might be upset at all those things I said when I was high, but they were understanding and even affable. I was at ease and comfortable enough to make a playful remark, "If you beat me at bowling I'll shave my head." I was going to add, "and run around the block naked," but I thought better of it at this early juncture

"Alright," she smiled. "Mom? Say goodbye to the nice young bald man."

Mrs. Seznick laughed and said goodbye as we were on our way to the alleys in yet another American monster—the Seznick station wagon.

Well, let's see, what excuse could I possibly give for being smoked three games in a row by this sweet young lady. Oh yea, "I'm heavily medicated, babe!" Actually we tied the last game at 118 but I had to strike out to do it. She was a lot of fun and I would have loved to take her out again, but I'm sure her boyfriend wouldn't approve and it's never been my style to be a home wrecker. I'm just glad that occasionally I'm blessed enough to meet people like her. There was a damn good reason why she was the object of my affection during the manic state—she was that good! I'm glad I had the chance to know her. To top off her niceness, she insisted that I didn't shave my head. She said that I was too cute and there was definitely a girl waiting around the corner for me.

And that's the way I'll always remember her.

Chapter Nineteen

Well, Donna Seznick was right, there was a girl right around the corner for me and man was she beautiful. I was sitting in the TV room one night late in December when I saw this girl walk by in the corridor and down to the girl's room. She was wearing a beige bathrobe, exactly like mine, and when she walked past, I was convinced that I knew her. I thought, and thought, when it came to me; she was Maureen McDonald, Tommy McDonald's (a friend of mine in M.U.N.) little sister who I had met briefly, once, in a bowling alley a year earlier. I ran over to the main board in the corridor and saw the name at the bottom, "Maureen McDonald." As I was reading this, she came up to me and said, "Hi" with a big smile on her face and walked rapidly past me. I turned around and called to her, "Wait! I know you, aren't you Tommy McDonald's little sister?" She turned around and looked at me inquisitively, "Do I look little to you?" She was short and she was skinny, so I surmised that she was referring to her not so petite—alright! Alright! She was buxom and obviously not shy about drawing attention to that fact. After all, it was the first thing she said to me except for "hi" in the bowling alley the previous year.

Now, I wouldn't say that this was love at first sight because it was much more like lust at first sight. Although my mania was gone, there were still residuals of that hypersexuality that goes with the disorder. Not to mention, again, that I was sixteen years old. She didn't remember meeting me at the bowling alley and I can't really say I blame her, I'm not that notable in a young, beautiful woman's eye. Short, skinny, shy at first, yellow teeth—the guy most likely to go nuts because he's smart enough to know that none of the "studs" these young girls are looking for are any smarter or any better than him at sports. So, she didn't remember me back then. The question becomes, will she ever forget me now that she's been hospitalized with me?

"How do you know me?" she was surprised.

"I met you in the Fountain Bowl with Elizabeth Machumis." Elizabeth was Tommy's girlfriend.

"There's a name I haven't heard in a while. How is the old girl?" The girl was grinning from ear to ear. Either she was goofy or she wanted a piece of the Archman. I immediately assumed she was goofy.

"I don't know," I sheepishly smiled back, "I've been in a mental hospital for a month and a half." She continued to smile at me and then did something completely unexpected—she walked away from me, down the hall, and into the girl's dorm room. Intriguing. Very, very intriguing. I shook my head at this and bounded my way down to the school where I listened to a CARS album and wrote a letter to my cousin Mark in the far corner of the school room. Since Linn Sue had gone, I didn't hang out with too many of the other kids. Julie and me became better friends and I got along well enough with the other guys—except Tony—but I was getting a touch depressed without a tight buddy. Then, that intriguing Maureen came into the schoolroom and made a bee line right to the corner where I was sitting with a distinct reason that I was not privy to. I stood up and tried to stand my ground (I swear Mom, I tried to get the hell out of the way but I was cornered and she was too fast) but this girl did not hesitate as she threw herself lips ablaze, upon my stunned, hopelessly inert body and mouth. She threw her arms around me and held me tight as I reciprocated, thinking to myself, "So that's how you do it . . . run straight at someone lips first." We made out for a couple of minutes until we heard someone coming and then we broke apart. She beamed at me ecstatically, "Hey, what's your name?" I took her right hand, making sure that Dave, who had seen us and turned around back down the corridor, was indeed gone, "My name is Archie McRae . . . It's nice to know you Maureen McDonald," and then I made out with her until Lana, one of the techs, caught us and reintroduced me to the infraction board. It was well worth the reprimand. It was well worth the reprimand. Oh, my God I can't stop saying that! It was well worth the reprimand. It was well worth the reprimand!

Now, the cast of characters changed over the course of my stay in the hospital, but one thing remained throughout—there were always couples. What could anybody possibly expect? For the most part, the relationships were short lived, life during wartime relationships, but the relationship I had with Maureen was different. First of all, her father, who met me at the pooh bah meetings, flat out liked me. I suppose Tommy also put in a good word for me. Anyway, he liked me so much that he decided to transfer Maureen from Huntington Beach High (she was living with her mom down old Huntington way by the beach) to Ocean View—and to let her come back and live with him, if that's what she wanted. Her history is a story in itself and I don't have time to get into it here, because more importantly to this text, when she told me all of this, the pressure was put on me. I was now the official boyfriend who everyone was looking at as being a positive influence on the "troubled Maureen" who was right next to me frantically bailing out the water of the sinking canoe known as our lives. This was not a good thing to do to someone, particularly a kid, who had just had a severe nervous breakdown. Of course, me being "the man" and all, I denied that this information bothered me. In fact, I thought it was great that Maureen would be going to my school when she was out of the hospital. But something deep down kept telling me that what Linn Sue had said about letting go of the experience, was right. Maybe the best way of dealing with the whole thing was to separate the experience from what went on outside the hospital before and after the experience. But I rapidly became involved with this girl. And then my wild imagination and phenomenal ability to project into the future seized me . . . what if: she and I were to go to school together, be lovers, go to college, get jobs and careers, be lovers, move in together, be lovers, get married, be lovers, have a kid, be lovers, raise the kid, be lovers . . . and then have to answer, "in a mental hospital," when the child asks where mommy and daddy met.

Although my doubts about this relationship ran rampant through my still over loaded mind, I let the physical part of the relationship blossom. I mean, we were just kids and all, and there was a chance we'd stay together, so I wasn't doing anything wrong by having fun with her. We'd sneak long, passionate kisses all over the place: in the school room, in the back visiting room, in the laundry room, in the linen closet, in the janitor's closet. We got away with it too, except for one time Cliff nailed us in the school room. Cliff was one of the coolest people I think I've ever met and he just cleared his throat, caught our attention, made a face of disappointment, smiled and then walked out of the room. We laughed and resumed our fun.

When good, and time permits, you were allowed half hour passes on the grounds. You could go down to the other buildings in the hospital such as the gift shop or the cafeteria. Or you could walk around the grounds, bask in the California sun and check out the lawns and gardens. When Linn Sue left, I would just walk around, lonely and depressed, and watch people in blue scrubs, run all over the compound. I thought to myself how wonderful it would be to wear those blue scrubs and be important. Then I would doubt that I could ever be important. I'd lower my head and continue on my half hour sojourn to nowhere until one time while I was walking around the abandoned old lab adjacent to the elevated 5 freeway, I saw it. The perfect place to make love to a woman. There was a tiny pond and bushes surrounding the pond, and a perfectly mowed patch of grass right next to this laboratory that was obviously abandoned. I fantasized about throwing a blonde on the grass and making mad passionate love to her for 27 minutes. I smiled and then fantasized the same with a brunette; a red head, a Chinese girl, a black girl, an Italian. Hey, I'm an equal opportunity fantasizer.

So I stored this valuable information in the back of my perverted little head thinking that maybe that's where I was going to lose my virginity. Why I thought this was beyond me, but I definitely felt that the grass by the little pond would be a good place to make the big score, ring the bell, hit the jackpot, see the sky rockets, bark with the dogs, you know—screw.

Maureen had to wait a week before she could go out on a grounds pass and I truly didn't take my little fantasy seriously, but when she did go on her first pass, which she did so three minutes after me (two patients can't leave together), I showed her the sights, conveniently leaving Archie's golden pond as the last stop. Holding her hand, I led her around the bushes and tackled her onto the soft patch of grass as she ecstatically shrieked and called my name, "Archie!!?" I can still hear that girl's laugh in my head as I peppered her with curt, peppy kisses of genuine affection. "You're a freaking lunatic!!" she laughed.

"Yea, ain't it great?"

"You're getting me all dirty you bastard," she was laughing as hard as I heard her laugh while I was directly on top of her with my face inches from hers. I let her calm down a bit, and when I saw her smile I kissed her passionately for a few minutes and then I reached down and unhooked the right strap of her green overalls and then the left strap. She displayed absolutely, positively, no resistance as I was making my bold move. I then kissed a bit as I fumbled around trying to take her top off, and then I had to have made the stupidest move in the history of romance—I looked at my watch!

"Jesus, Archie!!" I let go of the soft skin on her side by her hip, "what time is it?!"

"Oh, my God! It's 3:30!" she then pushed me off of her, and we both got up and started running as fast as we could, around the building down the driveway, past the volleyball court, up the ramp, through the doors and around the corner to the elevator doors. All eyes were on us as we panted profusely, waiting for that stupid elevator to come. When it finally did, we jumped in and pushed the button for the third floor. And resumed my passionate love assault on this beautiful creature that God had thrown in my path. There was plenty of time! Thirty seconds to a horny sixteen year old is like . . . what? four years to an eighty year old? We finally heard the ding and raced around the corner to the big metal doors. Panting, I picked up the phone and my innards rejoiced when it was Cliff who picked up the phone and came down to get us. We were a good 7-10 minutes late and that meant infractions for both of us, which meant no weekend passes for either of us, which meant no brief escape from the doors from hell, which was all of the patients number one priority at this juncture of our tragic, young lives.

Cliff turned around the corner and immediately displayed in inquisitive countenance; a face the likes of which heretofore I had never seen on the man's face. A facial expression I'll never be able to forget. He was walking quite slowly to the door, flat out staring through the glass door at Maureen whose overalls were drooped to her waist, her pink T-shirt was all over the place and not tucked in and her beautiful, straight, light brown hair was more than disheveled and resembled the do of the legendary Medusa. She, as well as I, were both panting heavily as Cliff stood staring at us and shaking his head slowly, oh, so slowly, two feet from the door.

"Come on Cliff, let us in." I was begging.

He looked at his watch and cleared his throat and smiled at me. He then nodded in Maureen's direction, "That's not exactly how the young lady left, you know." Ohh! look at that! Maureen was a mess. Well? How did she get like that? Beats me, officer. She put herself back together frantically and I continued to beg to get back onto the ward for no reason. I knew he wasn't going to give us an infraction.

"What's the magic word?" he smiled.

"Eat shit!" I smiled back.

"That's not it!" he smiled broadly . . . and then Maureen kissed the glass and laughed.

"That's more like it." All of us laughing, he let us onto the ward.

Chapter Twenty

When I look back on this first hospitalization, I think of a lengthy chunk of time in which I had absolutely, positively no control. The most valuable lesson I think I ever learned in my life was that there is no such thing as perfection in any way shape or form. Things can always be better and things can be worse. There is infinite outer space and infinite inner space. Trying to control everything is futile and leads to a life of misery. I learned this through the school of hard knocks at the age of sixteen. A raging river of questions filled my head when I was sixteen, as they still do today. Of course, the answer to all of these questions is a simple one—there is no such thing as perfection. Why did all of this happen to me when all my life, I tried to be good and never meant harm to anyone? Why is it that so many wonderful people suffer for no reason, when snakes in the moral pasture are looked upon as being great, God-like superstars who reap the fruits of success and turn their success into wealth and power? Why was there such a thing as luck? Why did I have bad luck?

At the age of sixteen I learned how truly unimportant I was and it was my new task in life not to take life as seriously as I had previously. This breakdown and illness made me both weak and strong . . . fragile and tough . . . nice and mean . . . happy and sad . . . quiet and loud . . . shy and bold . . . relaxed and tense . . . futile and omnipotent—ad infinitum. This was it, this was me. And despite the help of medicine, a war-like struggle was and always will be ahead of me, and there is no guarantee that I won't wind up in the hospital again (I've proven that point). The depressions are positively ruthless, particularly when you have to work through them and the manics are frightening despite how "fun" people think it is to be that happy and funny. The truth is, the manic is always at least a touch worried during these times because of an inability to stop and past experiences of disastrous manic highs that have simply destroyed their lives. Fun. Fun. Fun. So if you see me and I'm not smiling, it just means I'm trying to keep a touch depressed so that I don't have the manic explode in my face. The key to this is a substantial amount of sleep, (9 hours . . . naps included) despite what "normal" people advise you. The diet should be healthy and there really should be no alcohol, although I'm guilty of being painfully Irish. I don't want to be a hypocrite, and believe me, I'm not, so I'll tell you that I have been known to drink to excess and my diet has been junk for many years. I smoked 2-1/2 packs a day for ten years. So those pieces of advice come from someone who's been down the road of destruction and there is no guarantee that I might not fall back into a bad habit. There are no guarantees of anything in this life and that was a tasty morsel that was spoon fed to me for no apparent reason when I was sixteen.

Obviously I described the entire experience, or the most important aspects, but I haven't described what it was like writing all of this. It was a comforting outlet even if it's never published or even read. For starters, the reason I write is that it's a compulsion of manic depression known as hypergraphia. The reason I choose the topic itself was because I felt it necessary to inform people because the mentally ill are misunderstood and are still stigmatized. This text is not a doctor's description, this is what it's like. This bulky piece of writing is an attempt to be understood and to relieve the tension and fear that many people have concerning the subject. It's okay to be built differently than others, just hang tough. We're all here for a reason.

I feel much, much more relieved now that I'm done—it only took fifteen years to write the son of a gun (there's plenty of stories governing that statement—life has a funny way of getting in the way).

Thank you for reading and I apologize for the sharp language if you are sensitive to such slang.

I think I'll end on an inside joke that I myself just created.

How many manic depressives does it take to change a light bulb?

It doesn't make a difference, just make sure the damned bulb is fluorescent!

About the Author

Stephen Denis Manning is a graduate from the University of California at Irvine with a Bachelor of Arts in the discipline of Psychology. He has worked several years in the mental health/mental retardation field. This is Stephen's first novel although he has had several poems published.